澄清聲明

親愛的讀者：

倍斯特出版事業有限公司鄭重聲明，大陸中國紡織出版社與本社無業務往來。

近來發現本社之公司Logo，出現於中國紡織出版社之貝斯特英語系列書籍，該出版社自 2012年11月1日起之所有出版品與本社並無任何關係；鑑於此事件，懷疑有人利用本社之商業信譽，藉此誤導大眾，本社予以高度關注。特此聲明，以正視聽。

倍斯特出版事業有限公司 敬啟

倍斯特出版事業有限公司
Best Publishing Ltd.

胥淑嵐 · 著

上班族英語 The Essential Equipment To
English At Your Career

生存關鍵術

全民力拼生涯大突破　踏出關鍵的這一步
用專業英語勝出！

職場常用的單字：收納職場常用關鍵字，提供扼要的說明與例句，讓你學以致用。

現學現用的英語對話：主題對話為上班族必定出現的情境，內容符合職場需求。

實用應答小撇步：將同一情境可使用的不同英語句子，以條列的方式呈現，學習更豐富、表達的更為貼切。

經常遇到的討論話題：精選出現頻率極高的職場英語對話，讓你可以馬上學、馬上用。

多元化練習題：透過多元化且輕鬆有趣的學習方式，強化你的學習效果與應用能力。

特助行政秘書公關
內勤人員必備

作者序

　　台灣是一個島嶼型國家，與世界各國做貿易成為許多企業或個人，找出路、找活路的一種方式；於是乎，商務英語的重要地位誕生。但是除了貿易，上班族培養職場英語力也不容忽視；英語說得好，不但升遷有望，連帶薪水也跟著水漲船高。

　　「上班族英語生存關鍵術」根據我親身工作經歷，編寫了多種辦公室場景與對話，涵蓋職場中的各式情境，可以在最短時間，幫助職場人士找到適合的用語；不但增加英語能力，更可以順利成為老闆的得力助手！

　　Taiwan is an island nation, and doing trading with other countries in the world provides enterprises or single person an opportunity to survive.　Therefore, business English became important for Taiwanese.　Not only businessmen in trading business, but also people in other workplaces need to learn business English.　Speaking English fluently helps to get a promotion as well as a raise.

　　"The Essential Equipment To English At Your Career!" is written based upon my personal work experience which includes multiple office scenes and conversations, which allows readers to find appropriate sentences in a shorter time.　This book will not just help you to improve your English competency, but also help you to become your boss' right hand man!

編者序

　　這是一本實用務實的職場英語學習書。我們希望幫助讀者學習到切身會用到的 Live 場景英文，因而設計的每一個單元，都是針對職場的需要而來。特別是針對某些讀者相關，卻苦於沒有合適的書籍可以讓其學習到該場景的對話範例，本書可以協助您解決這樣的困擾，幫助您在更多元的語言學習對話場景中，體會到如何使用本書所提供的對話，在多元化的辦公場景，有效的談話與溝通。本書也有「實用應答小撇步」單元，幫助讀者學習有關類似的表達語意，卻有著不同的表達方式，既有趣又可以學習到許多實用的表達語句。您可以跟著本書的腳步，學會生活中不可或缺的職場情境對話。紮實而有趣，使您經由反應現實職場工作生活與生動活潑的對話，進入豐富的英語職場學習世界中。

倍斯特編輯部

目 次

Part One 致電

Part Two 抱怨處理

Part
One

致 電
Making a Call

Unit 01 致電客戶 Calling Clients

對話 1 Conversation 1

Kimberly	ABC Electronics Corporation. May I help you?	ABC電子公司。有什麼可以為您效勞？
Jack	Yes. Mr. Robins, please.	你好。請幫我接羅賓斯先生。
Kimberly	I am sorry, but he has a visitor at the moment. ①	抱歉，他現在有訪客。
Jack	Could you ask him to call me when he is free? ②	可以請妳讓他有空時回我電話？
Kimberly	May I ask why you are looking for him?	請問您找他有什麼事情呢？
Jack	I am calling to inform him that his order will be late for few days ③ due to inclement weather conditions of the departure country. ④	我是打電話來通知，他的貨物會遲幾天抵達，由於出發國家的惡劣天氣影響。
Kimberly	OK, no problem. Anything else?	好的，沒有問題。還有其他事情嗎？
Jack	Could you also tell him that we are	也麻煩請妳轉告他，我們

	not able to quote on all the items he needs?	無法對他需要的所有商品報價。
Kimberly	Why not? ⑤	為什麼不行呢？
Jack	Because we don't supply the first and the last item.	因為我們不提供第一個和最後一個商品了。
Kimberly	That is really bad, but don't worry, I will let him know. ⑥ Does he know your office number?	這真是太糟糕了，但是別擔心，我會讓他知道的。他知道您的辦公室電話號碼嗎？
Jack	Yes, he does. But ask him to call my cell phone, since I am outside the office now.	是的，他知道。但是請他打我手機，因為我現在不在辦公室。
Kimberly	Sure, no problem. What's your cell phone number then?	當然，沒問題。您的手機號碼是幾號呢？
Jack	0999123456.	0999123456。
Kimberly	Would you slow down, please? ⑦	請您講慢一點好嗎？
Jack	Sure. 0-9-9-9-1-2-3-4-5-6.	當然。0999123456。
Kimberly	Thank you. I guess that's all then?	謝謝您。我想就是這些了吧？
Jack	Yes, that's all. Thank you for your help. Bye bye.	對的，就是這些了。謝謝妳的幫忙，再見。
Kimberly	Good bye. Wish you a nice day. ⑧	再見，祝您有個愉快的一天。

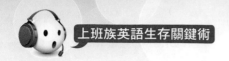

實用應答小撇步 1

① is not in right now / is out / is not at his(her) desk right now / is in a meeting now / is unable to come to the phone / hasn't come to the office yet

不在辦公室／外出了／不在座位上／正在開會／不方便接聽電話／還沒到公司

② call (me / you) back when he(she) is available

有空時回（我／你）電

③ will be canceled / will arrive early

將會被取消／將會提早抵達

④ postman strike / earthquake / volcanic eruptions / flight cancellation and delay

郵差罷工／地震／火山爆發／班機取消與延遲

⑤ May I know the reason... / Would you mind if I asking...

我可以知道⋯⋯的理由嗎？／你介意如果我問⋯⋯的話？

⑥ give him(her) your message / tell him(her) / inform him(her)

轉達留言給他（她）／告訴他（她）／通知他（她）

⑦ Please speak a little louder. / Could you speak up a little? / Would you speak more slowly?

請說大聲一點／能請您大聲一點嗎？／您介意說慢一點嗎？

⑧ Have a nice day.(afternoon, evening) / Have a lovely day.(afternoon, evening)

祝你有個愉快的一天（下午、傍晚）／祝你有個美好的一天（下午、傍晚）

對話 2 Conversation 2

Betty	Superman Trading Company. This is Betty Wu speaking.	超人貿易公司您好。我是吳貝蒂。
Su	Hello. May I speak to Edward, please? ①	妳好。請幫我接愛德華，謝謝。
Betty	I'll connect you now. ②	我現在就幫妳轉接過去。
Su	Thank you.	謝謝。
Betty	Sorry, no one answers.	抱歉，沒有人接聽。
Su	Can I have his extension number, please? ③	請問我可以知道他的分機號碼嗎？
Betty	I am sorry, but I think it's better if you try again later. ④	很抱歉，我想最好是妳稍後再打來。
Su	OK, I will. Thanks.	好吧，我會的。謝謝。
Betty	Bye bye.	再見。
	(15 minutes later)	（15分鐘後）
Su	Hi, could you put me through to Edward, please?	喂，麻煩幫我轉接給愛德華。
Betty	I am sorry, he is out. Would you like to leave any message? ⑤	真抱歉，他外出了。妳要留言嗎？

Su	All right. Please tell him that something urgent has come up, and our company would like to postpone the meeting until 12th.	好吧。請告訴他，因為一些緊急的事情發生了，我們公司希望延期會議到12號。
Betty	Please speak a little louder. You said until when?	請說大聲一點。妳剛才說幾號？
Su	We would like to POSTPONE THE MEETING UNTIL 12th.	我們想要延遲會議直到12號。
Betty	OK. I think I can hear you very well now. Is there anything else?	瞭解了。我想我聽清楚了。還有其他事情嗎？
Su	Please also tell him that the red one is no longer available.	也請轉告他紅色的已經不再供應了。
Betty	I'm sorry. I couldn't follow you. ⑥	抱歉，我不太懂妳的意思。
Su	He knows what it means. ⑦	他懂的。
Betty	All right, then. I will let him know.	那好吧。我會讓他知道。
Su	Thank you, bye-bye.	謝謝妳，再見。
Betty	Bye.	再見。

實用應答小撇步 **2**

① May(Can) I talk to / Can I speak to

我可以和……通電話嗎？

② I'll transfer this call / I'll put you through to (someone)/ I'll switch your call to (someone) / I'll put you through

替您轉接電話／我幫您轉給（某人）／我將轉接您的電話給（某人）／我將為您轉接

③ May I know his (her) extension (mobile, cell phone) number? / What's the number? / What's his (her) telephone (mobile, cell phone) number?

我方便請教他（她）的分機（手機）號碼？／電話號碼是幾號呢？／他（她）的電話（手機）號碼是幾號？

④ call back again / call back later

稍後再打來

⑤ Would you like me to take any message for you? / Would you like to give (someone) a message?

需要我幫忙留話嗎？／您要給（某人）留話嗎？

⑥ I'm not sure what you mean? / Could you put that in more specific terms? / Will you explain a little bit more? / I'm afraid I didn't understand that.

我不太確定您的意思／可以請您說得更明確一點？／您可以解釋一下嗎？／恐怕我沒聽懂（您的意思）

⑦ He gets that / He understands what it means

他懂的／他知道是什麼意思

💬 單字與句型

1. inform *v.* 通知
   A. inform + 人 + of / about + 物　通知某人某事
      I already informed Kelly of Paul's death.
      我已經通知了凱莉關於保羅的死訊。
   B. keep ... informed　隨時向⋯報告情況
      Please keep me informed about this case.
      請隨時向我報告這案子的情況。
   C. inform + against / upon / on + someone　舉報、舉發某人
      John decided to inform against his colleague after knowing he keeps stealing and selling company secrets to competitors.
      約翰在知道他的同事一直偷竊與盜賣公司機密給競爭對手後，決定要告發他。

2. due to　由於⋯的原因

3. inclement *adj.*　惡劣的
   也可以用 bad 取代。

4. be動詞 + able to　能夠
   If you are always too lazy to your homework, you will not be able to pass your exams.
   如果你總是太懶得寫作業，你就不可能通過考試。

5. quote *v.*　報價
   名詞為 quotation，報價單。

6. cancellation *n.*　取消
   此為名詞，動詞為 cancel。

7. extension *n.*　分機號碼
   此為名詞，也有擴充、延伸、續集、延期的意思。動詞為 extend。

8. urgent *adj.*　急迫的、緊急的

9. postpone *v.*　推遲、延期、暫緩、順延、改期

10. no longer　不再⋯
    形容詞，用在動詞前面。相似用法有 no more（副詞），用在動詞後面。
    They can no longer wait. = They can wait no more.
    他們不能再等了。

11. available *adj.*　可得的、合宜的、可用的

💬 練習題

A: Hi, Alice. I think this _____ doesn't sound reasonable.

B: What you want me to do?

A: Could you please _____ Mr. Wang that I need to talk to him about this.

B: Sure. But I don't have his _____ number.

A: You can ask David.

B: No problem. Anything else?

A: Also let Mr. Wang knows that the meeting can _____ wait, they must decide an _____ date.

B: OK, I will. But what if they want to _____ it?

A: Then we will be in big trouble!

A：嗨，愛麗絲。我想這份<u>報價</u>不太合理。

B：那你要我怎麼做呢？

A：可以請妳<u>通知</u>王先生我想要和他討論這件事？

B：沒問題。但是我沒有他的<u>分機</u>號碼。

A：妳可以問問大衛。

B：好的。還有其他事情嗎？

A：還有，也讓王先生知道這個會議<u>不能再</u>等了，他們必須要決定一個<u>合宜</u>的日期。

B：好的，我會的。但是萬一他們想要<u>取消</u>的話，怎麼辦？

A：那我們麻煩就大了！

💬 解 答

1. quotation　2. inform　3. extension　4. no longer　5. available　6. cancel

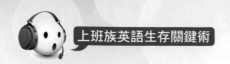

Unit 02

致電國外廠商
Calling Foreign Companies

對話 1 Conversation 1

Anna	ABC Corporate. This is Anna Chen speaking. How can I help you? ①	ABC企業您好。我是陳安娜。有什麼可以為您效勞的？
Vivian	Good morning. Please put me through to your President, please? ②	早安。麻煩替我將電話轉接給您們的董事長？
Anna	May I ask who's speaking, please? ③	請問您是哪位？
Vivian	This is Vivian Tsai of DEF Computer Company. I'm calling on behalf of Mr. Tom Ford, the general manager of our company. ④	我是DEF科技公司的蔡薇薇安。我是替我們總經理，湯姆福特先生致電。
Anna	Sorry, we have a bad connection here. ⑤ Could you repeat that, please? ⑥	抱歉，我們這邊收訊有點不好。可以請您重複一遍嗎？
Vivian	This is Vivian Tsai and I'm calling on behalf of Tom Ford, the General Manager of DEF Computer Company.	我是蔡薇薇安，替湯姆福特先生，DEF科技公司的總經理，致電。

Anna	Oh, OK. I can hear you now, but I am afraid that our President is in a meeting with the accountant at the moment, would you like me to take any message for you? ⑦	喔,好的。我聽見您了,但是恐怕我們董事長正在和會計開會,您想要我替您留話嗎?
Vivian	Sure. Please tell him that Mr. Tom Ford wants to talk about the mistake on our last invoice.	好的。麻煩轉告他,湯姆福特先生想要討論一下上回我們的報價單上的錯誤。
Anna	May I ask what about the invoice as well as how do you spell Ford?	我可以請教報價單怎麼了嗎,以及怎麼拚寫福特呢?
Vivian	I am not sure, but as I know it, we should have been given the large quantity discount.	我不是很確定,但是就我所知,我們應該被給予大宗訂購折扣才對。
Anna	I see. And your boss's last name, please?	了解了。那麼您的老闆的姓氏?
Vivian	Right, it's F-O-R-D.	對了,是F-O-R-D。
Anna	Perfect. I'll give him your message as soon as possible.	太完美了。我會盡早轉達您的留言。
Anna	You are welcome, bye.	謝謝妳。
Vivian	Thank you.	不客氣,再見。
Vivian	Bye-bye.	再見。

實用應答小撇步 1

① May I help you? / What can I do for you?

有什麼可以為您效勞？

② Could you connect this call with...? / Would you please connect me to... ?

麻煩替我轉接給…

③ Who is this, please? / Who's calling, please? / May I know who's calling?

請問是哪位？

④ I'm calling for...

我是替……致電

⑤ I can't hear you very well. / I can barely hear you. / I'm having trouble hearing you. / I can't catch what you are saying.

我聽不太清楚／我幾乎聽不見你說的話／我聽不清楚／我聽不太清楚你的話

⑥ Pardon? / Excuse me? / I beg your pardon? / Would you say that again?

抱歉，再說一遍好嗎？／抱歉，您說什麼？／能請您再說一遍嗎？

⑦ Would you mind calling back later?/ Would you like to give (someone) a message? / Would you mind holding the line? / Would you mind holding a little longer?

您介意稍後再致電？／您想要留言給誰（某位）嗎？／您介意線上等待嗎？／您介意稍等久一點？

對話 2 Conversation 2

Secretary	Good afternoon. Thomas Johnson's office. May I help you?	午安。湯瑪士強生的辦公室。有什麼可以為您效勞？
Hugh	Hello, is Mr. Johnson there? This is Hugh Morgan from ABC Trading Company.	喂，請問強生先生在嗎？我是ABC貿易公司的休摩根。
Secretary	Hello, Mr. Morgan. I'm sorry but Mr. Johnson is in Beijing on business. [1]	您好，摩根先生。很抱歉強生先生去北京出差了。
Hugh	May I know when he'll be back? [2]	請問他何時回來？
Secretary	I think it's this Friday.	我想應該是這個星期五。
Hugh	I cannot wait until this Friday. Is there anyone else who can help me? [3]	我不能等到這星期五。還有其他人可以協助我嗎？
Secretary	May I know your problem is first, so I can find someone else to help?	我方便先請教您的問題，然後找其他人協助您？
Hugh	Thank you. Your delivery cost is too high for me, not to mention the color of samples you sent to my office are totally wrong.	謝了。你們的運送成本對我來說太高了，而且你們寄來的樣品顏色全都錯了。
Secretary	I am really sorry for any	對於造成您的不方便，我

	inconvenience this might have caused you. ④ Mr. Johnson is the only one who's in charge of quotation. ⑤ As the sample problem, I think I can help in sending you the colors you need.	深感歉意。強生先生是唯一負責報價的人。至於樣品的問題，我想我可以幫忙寄送您所需要的顏色。
Hugh	That would be great! I need pink, cream, blue and purple.	太好了！我需要粉紅色、奶油色、藍色和紫色。
Secretary	Cream color may need few days to get ready, would you mind waiting? ⑥	奶油色可能需要幾天時間準備，您介意等候嗎？
Hugh	Not at all.	一點也不介意。
Secretary	OK. May I have your number and the address, please? ⑦	好的。請問您的電話是幾號，還有地址？
Hugh	02-12345678. 3 Floor, Number 777, Section 5, Nanjing East Road, Songshan Distinction, Taipei City, Taiwan.	02-12345678。台灣台北市松山區南京東路五段777號3樓。
Secretary	No problem and I'll let Mr. Johnson contact you as quick as possible when he's back from Beijing.	沒問題，我會讓強生先生從北京回來後，盡快和你聯繫。
Hugh	Thank you, bye bye.	謝謝你，再見。
Secretary	Good bye, Mr. Morgan.	再見，摩根先生。

實用應答小撇步 2

① on a business trip to Beijing / left for Beijing on business until October 1st

到北京出差／到北京出差，要到10月1日回來

② When he will be back? / Do you have any idea when he'll be back?

他幾時回來？／你知道他幾時會回來嗎？

③ Is there someone else who can make a decision? / Can you find somebody else to help me?

還有其他人可以做決定嗎？／你可以找到其他人幫我嗎？

④ We are terribly sorry for any inconvenience. / Please accept our deepest apology for any inconvenience this matter has caused you.

我們很抱歉引起了任何麻煩／對於任何引起您的不便之處，還請接受我們最深的歉意

⑤ be responsible for...

負責…事務

⑥ Would you mind waiting for (another) 5 days (weeks)? / Would you mind canceling this item? / Would you mind if we give you another one?

您介意（多）等5天（週）嗎？／您介意取消這個商品嗎？／您介意如果我們給您換上另一個？

⑦ What's the number? / What's your telephone (mobile phone) number?

電話號碼是幾號？／您的手機號碼是幾號？

單字與句型

1. corporate *n.* 企業
   亦可置換為corporation。此處報上自己的公司名稱即可。

2. put... through 替…接通電話
   Please hang on and I'll put you through. 請勿掛斷，我將為您轉接。

3. president *n.* 董事長
   也有總統，主席的意思。

   The President of USA 美國總統

4. accountant *n.* 會計

5. invoice *n.* 報價單

6. large quantity discount *n.* 大宗訂購（數量）折扣

7. not to mention 更別提
   亦可置換為to say nothing of / not to speak of。後接名詞或動名詞。

   They cannot afford an apartment, not to mention a house with a beautiful garden.

   他們都買不起公寓了，更何況是一個有漂亮花園的洋房。

8. distinction *n.* 區
   原為分別、區別的意思，在此作為行政區域上的「區」。

9. business trip 出差，商務旅行

10. have any idea 知不知道
    也有「有沒有任何主意」的意思。

    Do you have any idea about how to bring more customers? 有任何如何吸引更多顧客的想法嗎？

11. apology 道歉，致歉
    此為名詞，動詞是apologize。

💬 **練習題**

A: Good afternoon. ABC Company. How can I help you?

B: Hello, this is Alex and I am _____ Mr. Wang.

Could you please _____ your President?

A: Sorry, she is _____ .

B: I see. Is there someone else who can make a decision?

A: Perhaps her secretary could help.

B: _____ her secretary?

A: One moment, please.

A：午安。這裡是ABC公司。有什麼可以為您效勞？

B：你好，我是艾力克斯，替王先生致電。可以麻煩你替我轉接給你們董事長？

A：不好意思，她到上海出差了。

B：好吧。還有誰可以做決定呢？

A：也許她的秘書可以幫忙。

B：請你替我轉接給她的秘書。

A：請稍後。

💬 **解　答**

1. calling for / calling on behalf of

2. put me through to / connect this call with / connect me to

3. on a business trip to Shanghai / left for Shanghai on business / in Shanghai on business

4. Could you connect this call with / Would you please connect me to / Please put me through to

Unit 03 致電其他主管／同事 Calling Other Managers and Colleagues

對話 1 Conversation 1

Carl	Good afternoon, Marketing Department.	午安，行銷部門。
Natalie	Hi, is this Carl?	嗨，是卡爾嗎？
Carl	This is he. May I ask who's calling?	是的。請問是哪位？
Natalie	This is Natalie from Sales Department, could you connect this call with Robert Lin? I think Phil wants to discuss some things with him. ①	我是業務部的娜塔莉，麻煩幫我轉接給林羅伯？我想菲爾（娜塔莉的主管）有些事情想要和他討論。
Carl	I'll see if he is available. ②	我確認一下他現在是否方便。
	(One minute later)	（1分鐘後）
Carl	Sorry, Natalie. His line in busy right now, shall I ask him to call you back when he is free? ③	抱歉，娜塔莉。羅伯正在忙線中，我請他有空時回電？

Natalie	Phil is not able to wait too long for that. Would you mind telling Robert?	菲爾可能沒辦法等他。請你轉告羅伯吧？
Carl	Sure. Hold on for just one moment so I can grab a pen and paper. ④	當然，等我拿一下紙筆。
Natalie	Are you ready?	好了嗎？
Carl	OK. Now, please. ⑤	好了，請說。
Natalie	Phil wants to see the design draft of the DM for the new product launch from your department.	菲爾想要你們部門針對新產品上市的DM設計稿。
Carl	I heard that we already faxed last week. ⑥	聽說上週已經傳真過去了。
Natalie	The fax isn't readable. ⑦	傳真好像看不太清楚。
Carl	I can send it again.	我重新傳一次。
Natalie	OK, but be quick. Phil wants to receive that in ten minutes.	好的，但是要快一點。菲爾想要在10分鐘之內收到。
Carl	I'll do it as soon as possible.	我盡快。
Natalie	Thanks, bye.	謝啦，拜。

實用應答小撇步 **1**

① talk with him / talk about some things with him

和他談話／和他談論些事情

② Let me see if he's(she's) here / I'll go get him(her)

我確認一下他（她）是否在這裡（在位子上）／我去叫他（她）

③ He's(She's) on another line at the moment / He's(She's) talking a long-distance call now / Sorry, the line is busy

他（她）正在講另一通電話／他（她）正在講一通長途電話／抱歉，電話佔線（忙線）中

④ Let me find a piece of paper to write it down / Just a second. I'll get a pen

讓我拿紙筆記下來／等等，我拿支筆

⑤ Go ahead, please / Please speak

請講（說、進行）／請說

⑥ already provided / sent by E-Mail already / already sent by post(express delivery)

已經提供了／已經寄E-Mail了／已經寄郵遞（快遞）了

⑦ Few pages of the fax are missing / We didn't receive the fifth page of your fax/ The fax seems hard to recognize (due to the letters are too small)

傳真少了幾頁／我們沒有收到你傳真的第5頁／傳真很難辨識（因為字體太小了）

對話 2 Conversation 2

Jacob	Hello, this is Customer Service Department.	客戶服務部門你好。
Nicholas	Is Demi there?	請問是黛咪嗎？
Jacob	I'm afraid you have the wrong extension number. ①	你打錯分機了。
Nicholas	Oh, I am sorry.	喔，真抱歉。
Jacob	That's OK. Hold a moment. I'll put you through. ②	沒關係，你稍等。我幫你轉接。
	(One minute later)	（1分鐘後）
Jacob	She's on sick leave today. ③	她生病請假。
Nicholas	Will she go back to work this afternoon?	那她下午還回來上班嗎？
Jacob	Maybe not. She probably goes home. ④ Why? ⑤	應該不會，她應該回家去了。怎麼了嗎？
Nicholas	It's just there are few pages of the document she provided are missing. ⑥ Besides, we don't need some of them.	她提供的文件少了幾頁。而且有些是我們不需要的。
Jacob	Hold on one second, let me write this down. You said you are?	等等，讓我記下。你説你是？
Nicholas	Sorry, I forgot to introduce myself.	抱歉，忘了自我介紹。我

	This is Nicholas from IT Department.	是資訊部門的尼可拉斯。
Jacob	What is your extension number?	你的分機是幾號？
Nicholas	256.	256。
Jacob	Anything else?	還有其他事情嗎？
Nicholas	Yes, but can only tell her.	有的，但是只能告訴她本人。
Jacob	I'll ask her to call you tomorrow.	那我請她明天打分機給你吧。
Nicholas	That is good, thank you. See you.	這樣很好，謝謝你。再見。

實用應答小撇步 2

① You must have the wrong number. / What number are you trying to dial? / Will you check the number again, please?

您一定是打錯了／請問您要撥幾號？／您可以再確認一下號碼嗎？

② Can you hold on, please? / He'll(She'll) be with you in a moment. / Could you hold on any longer?

您能稍等一會兒嗎？／他（她）馬上就來聽電話了／您能再稍待一會兒嗎？

③ She is (He is) absent because she(he) is sick today. / She's on maternity leave now.

她（他）今天請病假／她目前正在休產假

④ She(He) has gone home / She(He) has gone for the day / She's(He's) left for home today / go(es) home for rest / go(es) to hospital / go(es) to see the doctor

她（他）回家了／她（他）已經回家了／她（他）今天已經回家了／回家休息／去醫院／去看醫生

⑤ What's the matter? / Why you asking?

怎麼了嗎？／為什麼這樣問呢？

⑥ forgot to provide most of the documents / messed up with other documents

忘了提供大部份的檔案／和其他檔案混在一起了

⑦ can only let her(him) know / can only tell her(him) in person / You don't need to know / It's a secret

只能讓她（他）知道／只能當面告訴她（他）／你不需要知道／這是秘密

單字與句型

1. Marketing Department　行銷部門
2. discuss　*v.*　討論、談論
   discuss為及物動詞，後不可接with等介系詞。discuss + something + with somebody才是正確用法。
3. draft　*n.*　草稿、草圖
4. new product launch　新產品上市
   launch的動詞和名詞同形。作動詞時有發射、開展、發動、發起的意思；名詞則有發射、快艇的意思。此為延伸意思，表示新產品要在市場上發射（上市）。
5. long-distance　*adj.*　長途的、遠距離的
   遠距離戀愛就翻成a long-distance relationship。
6. express delivery　快遞
   express此為名詞，特別快的意思。
7. recognize　*v.*　辨識
   作動詞還有認識、認清、認出、意識到的意思。
   I couldn't recognize you with your new haircut!　你的新髮型讓我都認不出你來了！
8. introduce　*v.*　介紹、引薦、引進
   A. introduce + 某人／某事物 + to + 某人
      My brother introduced Jazz to me.　我哥哥介紹了爵士樂給我聽。
   B. introduce + 某事物 + into + 某事物
      Films were introduced into television programs in 1970's.　電影在1970年代被引進了電視節目中。
9. IT Department　資訊部門
   IT的全名為information technology。
10. absent　*adj.*　缺席
11. maternity　*adj.*　產婦的、孕婦的
12. messed up　弄糟、搞砸
    I hope I didn't mess up your homework.　我希望沒把你的作業弄亂。
    He had messed up his career this time.　這一次，他把工作搞砸了。
13. in person　當面、面對面

💬 練習題

A: Is Kelly there?

B: She is on _____ from this week. Why?

A: She _____ this document, so I want to _____ with her _____.

B: Maybe you can make a _____ call.

A: I don't think so.

B: Or you can send by _____ to her.

A: That's a good idea, thanks.

A：凱莉在嗎？

B：她這週開始請產假。怎麼了？

A：她把這份檔案弄亂了，我想當面和她討論。

B：也許你可以打長途電話給她。

A：這樣不好吧。

B：或者你可以寄快遞給她。

A：好主意，謝了。

💬 解　答

1.maternity leave　　2. messed up　　3. discuss　　4. in person

5.long-distance　　6. express delivery

Unit 04 致電駐台辦事處 Calling Taipei Office

對話 1 Conversation 1

Staff	Good morning, this is Australian Office Taipei. How can I help you?	早安,這裡是澳洲台北辦事處。有什麼我可以幫您的?
Rachel	Hello, this is Rachel Chang from ABC Trading Company and I am calling for my boss. Could you put me through to the person who is in charge of issuing passport, please? I think my boss just lost his and we need to apply a new one.	哈囉,我是ABC貿易公司的張瑞秋,替老闆來電。可以請你幫我轉接給負責辦理護照的窗口嗎?我想我老闆弄丟了他的護照而我們需要申請一個新的。
Staff	Hold on, please.	請稍候。
	(Thirty seconds later)	(30秒鐘之後)
Staff	Sorry to have kept you waiting. ① The person is off for few days. ②	抱歉讓您久等了。負責人休假去了。
Rachel	May I ask when he will be back in office? ③	請問他幾號上班?
Staff	I am not sure. Maybe you can try again few days later? ④	我也不確定。或許妳可以過幾天再打過來試試看?

Rachel	My boss is in urgent need, do you have the person's E-Mail box or cell phone number so I can contact with? ⑤	我老闆很急，請問有沒有他的E-Mail信箱或手機可以聯繫？
Staff	We cannot disclose that information. ⑥ It is better you call back later.	我們不能透露。最好還是妳過幾天打過來試試。
Rachel	This is very inefficient. ⑦	這樣很沒有效率。
Staff	All right, give me your contact information and I'll let the person contact you.	這樣吧，給我妳的聯繫方式，我請負責人與妳聯繫。
Rachel	Great! This is Rachel Chang, 0999-123456. Do you also need my E-Mail address?	太好了！張瑞秋，0999-123456。E-Mail信箱地址要嗎？
Staff	Yes, please.	好的，請說。
Rachel	rachel@abc.com.tw.	rachel@abc.com.tw。
Staff	Let me repeat that. It's 0999-123456, rachel@abc.com.tw.	我重複一遍，是0999-123456，rachel@abc.com.tw。
Rachel	That's correct. When will you call me back?	沒錯。你什麼時候會回撥給我？
Staff	I will let you know once I reached him.	一旦我聯繫上他，就會讓妳知道。
Rachel	Please make sure as soon as possible. Thank you.	請保證要盡快。謝謝你。
Staff	I'll see what I can do. Bye bye.	我試試看吧。再見。

實用應答小撇步 1

① Sorry to keep you waiting / Thank you for waiting sir(ma'am) / Have I kept you waiting?

抱歉讓您久等了／先生（女士），感謝您的耐心等候／我讓您久候了嗎？

② He's(She's) on vacation this week / He's(She's) on vacation until next Monday

他（她）本週休假／他（她）休假到下周一

③ when he(she) will come (back) to work?

他（她）什麼時候回來上班？

④ call back again few minutes(hours) later

幾分鐘（小時）後再打過來

⑤ This sounds urgent / This sounds no big deal / We are not in the hurry, please take the time

聽起來很急迫／這聽起來沒什麼（不是什麼重要的事）／我們不趕時間，請慢慢來

⑥ We refuse to disclose / We cannot provide (give) you that information / We are not allowed to talk about that

我們拒絕透露／我們不能提供你那個資訊／我們不能（不被授權）談論那件事

⑦ I cannot accept that =This is unacceptable / I need more help from you / Could you provide more possible ways (solutions) for me?

我無法接受／我需要更多你的協助／你可以提供我更多可能的（解決）方案？

對話 2 Conversation 2

Answering Machine	Thank you for calling American Institute in Taiwan. Please dial the number you wish dial, or press nine, waiting for the operator.	感謝您致電美國在台協會。請直撥分機號碼,或按九,由總機為您服務。
	(Press 9)	(按了九)
Operator	Hello, may I help you?	您好,有什麼可以幫您的?
Simon	Hello, may I speak to Tiffany, the person who is responsible for business visa?	喂,請幫我轉接給蒂芬妮,負責商務簽證的窗口。
Operator	I am sorry, she is no longer at here. [1]	很抱歉,您要找的人已經離職了。
Simon	Does anyone else take responsibility for this?	還有誰負責這件事嗎?
Operator	We haven't found the successor yet.	目前還沒有找到繼任的人選。
Simon	I have a business trip in America two weeks later, and it is impossible for me to go if I couldn't get a visa by then! I will end up of losing tens of millions of dollars if this happens. What do you suggest me to do? [2]	我兩周後就要出差到美國,如果沒有簽證的話,根本出不去!這會害我損失好幾百萬美元的生意。你建議我該怎麼辦?
Operator	Sir, please calm down. [3] You could prepare all the applicant documents and send them to our office address.	先生,請冷靜一點。請您先將申請的文件備齊,寄到我們辦事處的地址來。

Simon	To whom, please?	要寫誰收呢？
Operator	Just write Apply for Business Visa, and that would be fine.	請寫申請商務簽證，這樣就可以了。
Simon	All right. What documents I need to send?	好吧。要準備什麼資料？
Operator	Your passport, two two-inch photos, return tickets and the reservation in the hotel, invitation letter from the U. S. company, as well as the application form. Please send by express delivery, so we can receive soon.	你的護照、兩張兩吋的相片、來回機票與酒店的訂購證明、美國公司的邀請函、以及申請函。為了盡早讓我們收到，您最好用快遞的方式寄出。
Simon	Can you make it in two weeks? ④	兩周內可以辦得出來嗎？
Operator	We will do our best while we can't guarantee the result.	我們會盡力，但是不保證結果。
Simon	But you should take the responsible of not finding the successor. This is really ridiculous! ⑤	你們應該為沒有盡速找到負責人選負責。這真的很荒謬！
Operator	Please accept our deepest apology for any inconvenience this matter has caused you.	對於任何引起您的不便之處，請接受我們最深的歉意。
Simon	Forget about it. Just process it as soon as possible for me.	算了吧。請幫我盡快處理就好。
Operator	All right, we will try to prioritize your application. Wish you a nice afternoon.	好的，我們盡量替您優先處理。祝您有愉快的下午。
Simon	Thanks, bye.	謝了，再見。

實用應答小撇步 2

① She(He) left this company last month. / She(He) was transferred to our branch office in Tokyo.

她（他）上個月離開公司了／她（他）被調到我們位於東京的分公司了

② What do you suggest I do then? / What choice do I have? / Please suggest a solution for this situation

那你建議我該怎麼做？／我有哪些選擇？／請為這情況建議一個解決方案

③ chill out / take a chill pill / stay(keep, remain) calm

冷靜／冷靜一下／保持冷靜

④ Can you deliver it to our office by next Monday? / Can you E-Mail (Fax, send express to) me by three PM?

可以下周一送到我們公司嗎？／可以在下午三點以前E-Mail（傳真、快遞）給我嗎？

⑤ Are you kidding me? / That's absolute nonsense! / That's wildly exaggerated! / That goes too far!

你在開玩笑吧？／完全沒道理！／這太誇張了！／太超過了！

⑥ Never mind. / Let it go.

別介意／讓它去吧

💬 單字與句型

1. in urgent need 緊急需要
    urgent有緊急的、急迫的、強求的意思。在醫學上，urgent可解釋成急症。
    urgent patient 急症的病患，反義詞就是non-urgent（非急症病患）。

2. disclose *v.* 透露、洩漏、批漏
    He disclosed the truth to the most of shareholders last week .
    他上週洩漏實情給大多數的股東們。
    We refuse to disclose our customers' names and addresses.
    我們拒絕透露顧客的姓名與地址。

3. inefficient *adj.* 沒有效率的、不稱職的、效能差的
    an inefficient worker 不稱職的工人
    The factory closed because of inefficient management.
    這間工廠因為沒有效率的管理而關廠了。

4. contact information 聯絡資訊、聯絡方式
    例如：姓名、電話、傳真號碼、手機號碼、地址、E-Mail信箱…等資訊。

5. successor *n.* 繼任人選
    success是成功的名詞，字尾+or就有接班人、後繼人選的意思。

6. applicant document 申請的文件

7. branch *n.* 分公司
    本意是樹的分枝，引申為分公司、分會的意思。另外，標點符號中的分號也
    是這個單詞。

8. pill *n.* 藥丸
    take a chill pill，直譯為服下一顆冷靜的藥吧，就是叫人冷靜下來的意思。

9. exaggerate *v.* 誇大、浮誇

10. prioritize *v.* 優先處理
    此為動詞，名詞為priority。
    If you don't prioritize your life, you will never be successful.
    如果你不將人生排列優先順序的話，你永遠不會成功的。

🗨 練習題

- Please write down the _____ , and you will be contacted shortly.
- David is the new _____ as General Manager of Shanghai _____.
- We should _____ the _____ production line.
- Please do not _____ the information on _____ to other people.

- 請留下您的聯絡資訊，我們會盡快與您聯繫。
- 大衛是上海分公司的新繼任總經理。
- 我們應該優先處理沒有效率的生產線。
- 請勿洩漏申請文件上的資料給其他人。

🗨 解　答

1. contact information
2. successor
3. branch
4. prioritize
5. inefficient
6. disclose
7. applicant document(s)

主題 ① 致電 Making A Call

職場補給站：接聽英語電話的「眉角」

接聽電話，在職場上扮演著相當重要的角色。職場專家也指出，電話在職場上，是一種有效的溝通工具；它的特性有：低成本、即時性與互動性高、用聲音溝通，比**E-Mail**更能體現人性，也比視訊少了面對面的緊張感。其重要性不言可喻，言談之中的禮儀甚至會影響對方對公司的觀感與評價，或生意的成交與否。初入職場的新鮮人，對於公司前輩或者公司開課教授電話禮儀，應該有所印象；商務進修課程中，電話禮儀或電話溝通，也成為秘書或新進職場工作人的熱門課程之一。

用英語接聽電話和用中文一樣，有著幾點基本要求：

❶ 響三聲之內接起。曾經有統計指出，一般人對於等待電話被接起只有三聲的限度。假使無法在響三聲之內接起，開頭一定要補上：「抱歉讓您久等了(Sorry for keeping you waiting.)」，如此一來，打電話的人會知道你在意這通電話，心情也就不會太糟了。

❷ 微笑的語氣。聲音是有感染力的，千萬別以為隔著話筒，對方就無法感受到你的情緒；反而是因為沒有面對面，所以對於對方態度的唯一判斷來源─聲音，會特別敏感。要記得，代表公司接聽電話就是代表公司的形象，來電者可能是在外地的同事、出差的主管、要簽約的客戶，甚至是董事長，禮貌且帶有微笑的語氣，不但能讓接聽的人感到被尊重，也連帶對公司留下好印象。

❸ 勿同時做其他事情。有些職場人士認為自己是老鳥了，對於接電話心不在焉，可能同時和鄰座同事講話、整理桌面、看著電腦螢幕工作⋯等等，一時疏忽，可能錯過對方的重要訊息；職場專家也建議，不論是在什麼位

階，當有電話響起時，專注處理完再辦其他工作才是正確的態度。

但是英語畢竟不是母語，為了減少出錯，用英語接聽電話時，有幾點「眉角」（台語，意味重要的地方）要留意：

❶ 熟練重要關鍵句或單字。例如：我替您轉接、請稍後、他現在不在座位上、他出差了、我替您留言、我會請他回電給您。如果要知道各行業高頻率的電話句子，也可以請教公司或同行的前輩，記下並反覆演練。

❷ 隨時準備紙筆。由於英語並非我們母語，而且還有各國人講英語的口音問題，為了避免聽錯或者跟不上，接起電話前就要準備好紙筆，隨時記下關鍵字句。通常，你需要記下至少：來電者姓名（最好是全名，以防有同名的人）、聯絡方式、來電理由、特殊需求或協助事項（例如，需要在何時以前回電）。

❸ 最後不要忘記介紹自己。基於商務禮貌，如果來電者要找的人不在辦公室，而你是留言者的話，也不要忘記在最後用一句話介紹你自己，好讓對方知道是誰替他/她轉達的。通常可以説：我是＿＿＿＿我會保證＿＿＿＿會收到這則留言的。(This is ＿＿＿＿ and I will make sure ＿＿＿＿ will get this message.)

Part
Two

抱怨處理
Deal with Complaints

Unit 01 消費者抱怨 Consumer Complaints

對話 1 Conversation 1

Kate	Hi, Steve. Can I ask you something? ①	史蒂夫，我能問你一些事嗎？
Steve	Of course, what is it? ②	當然，什麼事？
Kate	You must see a lot of complaints at counters every day, aren't you? What do you do to calm them down?	你每天在專櫃一定見過很多抱怨吧？你是怎麼讓他們冷靜下來呢？
Steve	Some of them are reasonable, some just express emotions. So, first of all, you have to make a judgment about which kind of complaints they are making. Then listen attentively. ③	有些抱怨是合理的，有些只是情緒抒發。首先，你要判斷是哪一種抱怨，然後用心聆聽。
Kate	That's it? Listen attentively?	就這樣？用心聆聽？
Steve	It's important, sweetheart. ④ If the complaint is reasonable, then write it down and report to headquarter, this means your department.	這很重要呢，親愛的。如果是合理的，那麼就寫下來，報告給總公司，也就是你們部門。

46

Kate	What if they just give vent to someone?	如果他只是發洩呢？
Steve	Listen patiently, do not interrupt. [5] Then you make an apology. Remember, don't complain with them together, nor find excuses to shirk responsibilities.	那就耐心聽完，不要打斷。然後道歉就好。記得千萬不要和他們一起抱怨，也不要找藉口推卸責任。
Kate	What if it's not the company's fault?	萬一不是公司的錯呢？
Steve	Usually, consumers will assume it is mostly the company's fault. If not, just like I said, make an apology after listen patiently.	通常消費者會假設大部分都是公司的錯。如果不是我們的責任，就如同我說過的，聽完道歉就好。
Kate	This is it? No need to do something about it? [6]	就這樣？不用做點什麼嗎？
Steve	Maybe give some small gifts after that, you know, giveaways or coupons, etc.	也許事後送點小禮物，妳知道的，贈品、折價券等等。
Kate	Or some compensation?	或是一些補償金？
Steve	I am not sure, I think your department or General Manager will decide that.	這我就不太確定了，我想你們部門或總經理會決定吧。
Kate	I see, now I understand. Thank you very much. [7]	原來如此，現在我懂了。真謝謝你。
Steve	You are welcome, anytime.	不客氣，隨時候教。

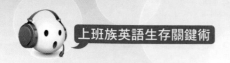

實用應答小撇步 1

① May I ask you few questions? / Would you mind answering some questions for me? / Would you mind if I ask you some things? / Can I ask you something personal?

我可以問你一些問題嗎？／你介意回答我一些問題嗎？／問你些問題，你不介意吧？／我能否問你些私人問題？

② Sure, go ahead / OK, shoot / Sure, please

當然，說吧（問吧）／好呀，來吧（問吧，說吧）／當然，請說

③ listen carefully / listen patiently / look at thoughtfully / look at me attentively

留心地聆聽／耐心地聆聽／仔細地看／注意聽我講話

④ It is serious / They are significant / It matters

這是要緊的／它們是重大的（重要的）／這有關係（這很重要）

⑤ Don't change the subject / Don't distract attention from we are discussing / Don't argue with customers

不要轉移話題／不要從我們正討論的事情上轉移注意力／不要和消費者爭論

⑥ Do nothing about it? / Let us compensate you for your expenses? / Do something!

不用做什麼（袖手旁觀的意思）？／讓我們補償您的花費（支出）吧？／幫幫忙，做點什麼吧！

⑦ Of course / That explains it / I understand

原來如此／這樣解釋就通了／我懂了

對話 **2** | Conversation **2**

Customer	Hi, I think there is something wrong with my notebook. Can you check it for me? [1]	嗨，我這台筆記型電腦有點問題。幫我看看好嗎？
Staff	Sure, what's the problem? [2]	什麼問題呢？
Customer	It takes long time to start it, and sometimes, it shutdowns automatically.	開機很久，而且有時候會自動關機。
Staff	Maybe some errors, that's all. Don't worry, we offer free maintenance during the warranty period. Do you have the receipt with you? [3]	應該是故障了。別擔心，只要是保固期間都可以免費維修。請問您有攜帶發票嗎？
Customer	No, I don't have. I bought it very long time ago.	沒有，很久以前買的。
Staff	OK, I can check that for you. I'm sorry, Sir. It has been three years and you need to pay for the maintenance yourself.	我幫您查一下。很抱歉，先生。你已經買三年了，需要自費維修。
Customer	This is ridiculous! [4] It should be the bad quality of the product, and I think the company needs to take the responsibility.	這太扯了！應該是產品品質不佳，公司應該負起責任來。
Staff	Sir, there are many causes of a	先生，故障的原因很多，

	malfunction in the computer, probably due to the misuse and it's out of our responsibility. I suggest you to send it for repair, if it still doesn't work, then you need to buy a new one.	可能是使用上的問題造成的，原本就不在公司擔保範圍內。我建議您送修，如果實在不行，可以買一台新的了。
Customer	I don't really want to change it. Before it has problems, it worked well. Besides, the data is all inside.	我還不想換，故障前使用起來很順手。此外，資料也還在裡面。
Staff	OK, I can help you to back up your data first.	這樣吧，我先幫您把資料備份起來。
Customer	Thanks. How much for today?	謝了。一共是多少錢？
Staff	This checking is free. The maintenance fee needs to wait until we send it for repair, and we'll call you. Please fill out the repair order form first. ⑤	今天檢查是免費的。但是維修要估價後才知道，會打電話通知您的。請先填維修單。
Customer	I hope it works, because I don't want to waste my money. ⑥	最好有效，我不想浪費錢。
Staff	Don't worry, you can decide whether you want to repair or a new notebook. ⑦	別擔心，您可以到時候評估要維修還是要買新電腦。

實用應答小撇步 2

① Would you give me a hand? / Could you do me a favor? / Do you need any help? / What can I do for you?

能幫我一把嗎？／麻煩你幫我一個忙？／需要任何幫忙嗎？／能為你做些什麼？

② Any question? / Anything wrong? / Is that a problem? / What's your problem?

有疑問嗎？／有問題嗎？／是不是有問題？／你到底有什麼問題？（通常是不耐煩質問對方你有什麼不滿）

③ Do you have the invoice? / May I have your credit card? / I need to see your ID, please

你有發票嗎？／能給我您的信用卡嗎？／麻煩你，我需要看你的身分證件

④ Unbelievable! / This can't be happening! / Not a chance! / No way

不可思議！／這不可能（發生）的！／門都沒有！／不行（不可能）

⑤ Please fill out our Customer Satisfaction Survey / Please fill out customer information form / Please contact out Customer Complaint Department

請填寫我們的顧客滿意度調查問卷／請填寫顧客資料／請聯繫我們的顧客申訴部門

⑥ Hope it's useful / It's not going to work / This is a workable plan / I have doubts about your suggestion

希望這是有用的／行不通的／這是一個行得通的計畫／我對你的建議有所懷疑

⑦ Don't you worry / No worries / No need to worry

擔心啦／沒問題（也有不客氣的意思）／不用擔心

單字與句型

1. counter *n.* 專櫃
   cosmetics counter in department store 在百貨公司的化妝品專櫃

2. express emotions 抒發情緒
   也可以寫成express feelings。

3. attentively *adv.* 留心地
   同義詞有carefully, cautiously, with consideration。

4. give vent to 發洩、宣洩
   Jack doesn't dare give vent to his annoyance in front of her parents.
   傑克不敢在父母面前宣洩他的煩惱。

5. shirk responsibility 推卸責任
   亦可寫成shirk away from responsibility。

6. giveaway *n.* 贈品

7. coupon *n.* 折價券

8. compensation 賠償金
   此為名詞，動詞為compensate。

9. personal *adj.* 私人的、個人的
   It's personal. 這是私人的事情／物品((請勿亂動的意思)；事關個人隱私（我不一定要回答的意思）。

10. shoot 說吧
    原意是射擊、發射的意思，動詞。在口語上引申為，請對方爽快發言、暢談的意思。

11. free maintenance 免費維修

12. warranty period 保固期間
    3-year warranty 三年保固

13. misuse *n.* 使用不當
    The manufacturers disclaim all responsibility for the damage caused by misuse. 製造商拒絕負擔所有因為不當使用而產生的損壞。

💬 練習題

1. It will be considered as unprofessional if you _____ your anger to your colleagues.

2. _____ are important to housewives.

3. The bakery tried to _____ to its suppliers.

4. ABC computer offers a _____ and _____ service to our worldwide consumers.

5. It is a _____ question, and I don't want to answer it.

1. 工作時把不滿發洩到同事身上會被視為不專業。

2. 折價券對家庭主婦們很重要。

3. 麵包店企圖推卸責任給上游廠商們。

4. ABC電腦提供全球消費者2年保固以及免費維修服務。

5. 這是私人的問題,而我不想回答它。

💬 解　答

1. give vent to

2. coupons

3. shirks responsibility (shirk away from responsibility)

4. 2-year warranty;free maintenance

5. personal

Unit 02 客戶抱怨 Client Complaints

對話 1 Conversation 1

	(At the Conference Room)	（在會議室裡）
Melody	Hello, Johnny. I am glad we finally meet. ①	嗨，強尼，很高興我們終於見面了。
Johnny	Me too.	我也是。
Melody	I hope you are satisfied with our services. ②	我希望您對我們的服務都還滿意。
Johnny	Actually, I am here to discuss whether we can have a better way of cooperation.	事實上，我是來和貴公司討論有沒有更好的合作方式。
Melody	No problem, please.	沒問題，您請說。
Johnny	We didn't get discounts for our orders, and since we have been cooperated for six months, I think maybe we should get some discounts.	之前我們訂貨都沒有優惠，我們合作半年了，我想應該可以享有優惠了。
Melody	We offer a discount for large orders, maybe you didn't reach a certain level of amount. ③	我們對大量訂貨有提供優惠，可能是您之前沒有達到一定的數量。
Johnny	I've never heard of such a thing! ④	這點我從來不知道！如果

54

	If this is so, we would order more.	是這樣，我們一定會多訂一點。
Melody	We are sorry for any inconvenience this matter has caused you. Didn't Lily explain to you before?	很抱歉造成您的困擾。莉莉之前沒有向您解釋嗎？
Johnny	This is your company's negligence ⑤ and I strongly request the changing of the contact person. ⑥	這是貴公司的疏失，我強烈要求更換聯繫窗口！
Melody	No problem, we'll give you an extra discount this time except the large order.	好的，這次訂購除了大宗優惠以外，我們再給予折扣。
Johnny	That's more like it. ⑦	這還差不多。
Melody	Anything else I can do for you?	還有任何我可以幫得上忙的地方嗎？
Johnny	I am wondering if the delivery addresses are different, can we have discounts.	如果運送地點是不同的話，運費上可不可以給予優惠？
Melody	It's not possible based on your past orders, but if your orders reach a certain level and then yes, we can do what you request.	依照您以往的成交價格是不可以的，如果達到一定的金額以上，我們可以依照您的需求處理。
Johnny	Perfect! Then that's everything. May we have a pleasant cooperation.	太好了。那麼就這樣吧，希望以後合作愉快。
Melody	Thank you very much for your visiting today. Wish us a good cooperation.	非常感謝您今日的拜訪，祝我們合作愉快。

實用應答小撇步 1

① I am glad we finally got the chance to meet / It was glad to meet you / Great to finally meet you!

很高興終於有機會見面了／之前（昨天或更早以前）很高興與你見面／終於見到你了！

② We hope you will be satisfied with the level of service we provide / Are you (not) satisfied with our service?

我們希望您將會對我們提供的服務滿意／您（不）滿意我們的服務嗎？

③ We can make the price lower if you would order a bit more / We can offer a 10% discount for orders over 5,000 pieces

我們可以降價，如果您多訂一些／訂購5千個以上，我們可以提供10%折扣（九折）

④ I have never been told / I have never seen such appalling behavior / I have never thought like that / We have never expected you will be treated like this

我從來沒聽過（沒被告知）／我從來沒見過這麼惡劣的行為／我從來沒有這樣想／我們從來沒有想到您會被這樣對待

⑤ It is (not) the firm's responsibility / We hope your company could compensate us in some ways

這（不）是公司的責任／我方希望貴公司能以一些方式賠償我方

⑥ I would strongly recommend replacing the contact person / I suggest you change David with John / I think you should do the work yourself / Who would you recommend?

我強烈建議更換聯繫人／我建議你把大衛的工作換成約翰來做／我覺得你應該親自做這工作／你建議誰來做？

⑦ Now you are talking / That's what I am talking about

這才像話嘛（你說中了）／這就是我說的意思（這就是我剛才提到的）

對話 2 Conversation 2

	(At Exhibition)	（在展會上）
Allen	Hi, Owen. What a surprise to meet you here in Hong Kong Exhibition?	嗨，歐文，你怎麼也來參加香港的展會呢？
Owen	Yap, my company sent me on a business trip. Since I met you here, there is one thing I want to make a complaint about. ①	是呀，公司派我出差。正好在這裡遇見你，我有件事情想向你抱怨。
Allen	Yes, please.	什麼事？你請說。
Owen	It's about the samples you sent last week, their sizes and colors are all wrong. ②	關於你們上週寄來的樣品，尺寸和顏色都弄錯了。
Allen	Oh, my God. I cannot believe it!	我的天啊，真不敢相信！
Owen	It's true. You may need to resend them as soon as possible. ③	是真的。可能要盡快重寄一次。
Allen	I'll ask my colleagues to deal with right now, and you will receive them the day after tomorrow. ④	我馬上請同事處理，後天就讓你們收到。
Owen	One more thing, can your company pays for the shipping fee of sending samples? ⑤	還有，寄送樣品的運費可不可以由你們公司買單？
Allen	For the wrong sending, yes. But not for the other conditions, I am	寄錯的當然由我們負責。但是，其他情況下恐怕不

	afraid.	行。
Owen	Well, since we have been cooperated for a long time. Besides, what among same trade is the shipper will pay for the sample shipping costs once customers ordered.	我們合作這麼久了，而且同業的作法是，如果之後下訂的話，樣品的運費可以由出貨方來負擔。
Allen	I will report it to my boss. ⑥ However, I cannot guarantee the result.	我會向公司反映。但是，不能給你保證結果。
Owen	In this case, we will consider finding other companies. ⑦	這樣的話我們會考慮找其他公司合作。
Allen	Please, Owen. I will do my best to convince my boss.	別這樣，歐文。我會盡力說服老闆。
Owen	All right, please do so. That's all, I am going to walk around.	好吧，那就麻煩你了。先這樣，我還要去逛逛呢。
Allen	OK. Hey, how about let's go for a drink tonight?	好的。晚上一起喝一杯吧。
Owen	If it is your treat.	你請客我就去。
Allen	No problem!	那有什麼問題！

實用應答小撇步 2

① I want to file a complaint against a business / I want to report a lying colleague to my boss / I want to tell you a secret

我想對一家公司提出申訴／我想向上司舉報一位說謊的同事／我想告訴你一個秘密

② The last shipment was not up to par / The quantity was not correct / There is a mistake on last time's invoice / Your price seems a little higher　上次送來的貨未達標準／送來的貨數量不對／上次的發票有一個錯誤／你們的報價似乎比較高

③ Please adjust quickly / I hope you can provide soon / I'll get back to you later　請盡快修改／希望盡早提供／我將會晚點回覆你

④ I'll get on it immediately / I am on my way / I'll be right with you / She will transfer the money by the weekend / We cannot wait any longer

我馬上去辦／我馬上就到了／我馬上就回來＊／她週末前就會去匯款／我們不能再等了　＊可用於電話中，也可用於面對面會議時

⑤ Can you pay for the sample charge (courier charge)? / Can you send me some catalogs (samples) free? / Could you make the price lower for me?

打樣費（快遞費）可不可以由你們負擔？／可以免費提供型錄（樣品）嗎？／報價可以再便宜一點嗎？

⑥ I will let my company knows your concern / I will report to my boss / Please provide your feedback to us / Please feel free to express(convey/give) your opinions to us

我會讓公司知道您的顧慮／我會向上級報告／請提供您的寶貴意見給我們／請隨時表達您的意見給我們

⑦ We will cancel the deal if you persist in doing this / I will see you in court if you keep running away from your debt

我們將會取消合約，如果你堅持這樣做／你再繼續欠債不還的話，我們法庭上見

💬 單字與句型

1. conference room *n.* 會議室

2. cooperation *n.* 合作
   同義詞還有collaboration、teamwork、coordination。

3. negligence *v.* 疏忽、疏失
   同義詞還有neglect、careless、oversight。

4. contact person 聯繫人、聯繫窗口
   contact(s)或contact information也是常用來表示聯繫窗口、聯繫資訊的詞。要注意的是，contact window在台灣常用來表示聯繫窗口，但是並非正確英語。

5. complaint *n.* 抱怨
   除了make a complaint的用法以外，「我要抱怨、客訴」還有另一種講法：file a complaint。
   He filed a complaint against his neighbor for making noise all day long. 他對鄰居因為整天製造噪音而提出抱怨。

6. same trade 同業
   也可寫作same business。
   We are from same trade. 我們是同業。

7. not up to par 未達到標準
   為高爾夫球術語，指沒有達到標準桿數（意即在水準以下），延伸指一般未達標準的情況。要注意的是，這句並沒有肯定句(up to par 達到標準)的用法。

8. invoice *n.* 發票
   完整單詞為Commercial Invoice，商業發票。
   To issue/make/create the invoice 開發票

9. catalog *n.* 型錄
   也寫作catalogue。

💭 練習題

A: Hi, Julia. This _____ seems has a problem.

B: What is it?

A: It doesn't include the fee of _____ we sent to your _____ last week.

B: Oh my God! It is my _____ .

A: It's OK, just issues another one.

B: Thank you for your reminding. By the way, do you know where our boss is now?

A: He is in a meeting at _____ .

B: OK. My client wants to talk with him about _____ matters. See you around.

A：嗨，茱莉亞。這張發票好像有點問題。

B：是什麼呢？

A：它好像沒有把上週寄給你的聯繫窗口的型錄費用含進來。

B：我的老天！這是我的疏失。

A：沒關係，再重開一張發票吧。

B：謝謝妳提醒。對了，你知道老闆現在在哪裡嗎？

A：他在會議室開會。

B：好的。我客戶要找他談合作事宜呢。回頭見。

💭 解　答

1. invoice   2. catalog   3. contact person

4. negligence / neglect / careless / oversight   5. conference room

6. cooperation

Unit 03 其他主管／同事抱怨 Other Managers/Colleagues Complaints

對話 1 Conversation 1

Ivor	Hi, is Will there?	喂，威爾在嗎？
Katherine	I am sorry, but he is in a meeting right now.	抱歉，他現在正在會議中。
Ivor	OK. Could you ask him to call me back immediately when he finished the meeting?	好吧。可以請你讓他會議後立刻回我電話？
Katherine	I am sorry, but he will have the meeting this whole afternoon. [①]	很抱歉，他今天整個下午都在開會。
Ivor	What? OK, could you take a message, please? [②]	什麼？好吧，可以麻煩你幫我留個話？
Katherine	Sure. Just a moment, let me get my pen. [③]	沒問題。等等，我拿支筆。
Ivor	OK? Are you ready?	好了嗎？你準備好了？
Katherine	Yes, please.	是的，請說。
Ivor	We should receive the new products one week ago, but still waiting for them. Besides, the colors are all wrong, we do need	我們應該在一個星期前就要收到新產品，但是我們現在還在等它們。此外，貨物的顏色都錯了，我們

	an explanation here. ④	實在需要一個解釋。
Katherine	I promise he will get this. ⑤	我保證他會收到留言。
Ivor	Oh, right, what's the promotion event for Christmas? We haven't received any form of notification yet. What should we do to deal with poor performance?	對了，聖誕節促銷活動的內容是什麼？我們到現在都還不清楚。如果業績表現不好該怎麼辦？
Katherine	No problem, I will let him know. Is there anything else? ⑥	沒問題，我會轉達。還有其他事情嗎？
Ivor	No. Just let him call me as soon as possible. ⑦	沒有了。讓他盡快回電給我就是了。
Katherine	No problem. May I ask is this Ivor?	沒問題。請問您是艾佛嗎？
Ivor	Yes, that's me.	對，我是。
Katherine	OK. Sorry for the inconvenience caused by our department.	好的。對於我們部門引起的不便深感抱歉。
Ivor	It is very inconvenient! I have to say that your department is so inefficient.	的確是很不方便！我再次強調你們部門真是太沒有效率了。
Katherine	I am really sorry about that.	實在抱歉。
Ivor	All right, that's all. Let Will call me ASAP.	好啦，就這樣吧。讓威爾盡快給我電話吧。

實用應答小撇步 1

① is not in the office this morning / is at client's company all day / be on a business trip during the whole week / be overseas in a month

整個上午都外出／整天都在客戶那／整個禮拜都出差／整個月都在海外

② May I have a message? / Please put me through to his(her) secretary / tell him(her) I(you) called / Could you tell him(her) that...

可以替我留言嗎？／請幫我轉接到他（她）秘書那裡／轉告他（她）我（您）來過電話／請幫我告訴他（她）……

③ Hold on, let me get a pencil and paper / Hold the line, please. I'll get an English speaker / Please wait a second. I'll get someone to the phone

稍等，讓我拿支筆和紙／請別掛斷，我請會說英語的人來／請稍等，我請其他人來聽電話

④ We need someone to take responsibility for the actions / We need the apology from your company / They expect that somebody do them justice

我們需要有人為行動後果負責／我們需要你們公司的道歉／他們期待有人替他們主持公道

⑤ I guarantee he(she) will receive the package / I'll assure the delivery will be on time / I'll make sure the meeting will end before six PM

我保證他（她）會收到包裹／我會確保運送準時抵達／我會確保會議將在下午6點前結束

⑥ Is that all? / Is there anything else I can do for you? / What else do you need?

就這些嗎？／還有其他我可以幫你的嗎？／您還需要什麼協助嗎？

⑦ reply me email ASAP / send me back soon / report back to me early

盡快回E-Mail給我／盡快（郵）寄回給我／早一點回報讓我知道

對話 2 | Conversation 2

(At staff room)	（在茶水間）
Jacqueline Have you heard about it?	你聽説了嗎？
Paula What are you talking about?	什麼事呀？
Jacqueline Charles from the customer service department is complaining you all around the office. ①	客服部的查爾斯一直到處在抱怨妳耶。
Paula What? How could this happen? I don't remember I have offended him.	什麼？怎麼會這樣呢？我不記得我有得罪過他。
Jacqueline I heard it's because you didn't take his shift last week's PR event.	聽説就是上週的公關活動妳沒有幫他代班。
Paula That's because my schedule was full, I really cannot help him.	那次是因為我的行程滿檔了，真的幫不了他。
Jacqueline I don't get it either. Maybe he thinks he has personal grudge against you. ②	我也不清楚。也許他視為是私人恩怨。
Paula Jesus! He is so childish. ③	天啊！他也太幼稚了吧。
Jacqueline Maybe, but this will destroy your reputation soon. If he continues talking you like this, you will be in everyone's black books. ④	可能吧，但是妳的名譽就快被這事毀掉了。如果他再這樣傳下去的話，妳就會變成每個人心中的不受歡迎人物啦。

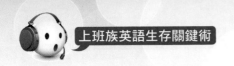

Paula	Then what should I do? ⑤	那麼我該怎麼辦好呢？
Jacqueline	First, ask Charles come out privately and explain the whole thing well. Ask him not to continue to spread anything behind your back.	首先，私底下找查爾斯出來解釋清楚，請他不要再繼續在你背後散播。
Paula	What if he doesn't listen to me? ⑥	如果他不聽呢？
Jacqueline	Report to your manager, then. Ask him to coordinate with Charles's manager. ⑦	上報妳的主管。請他和查爾斯的主管來協調囉。
Paula	Do you think it gonna work?	會有用嗎？
Jacqueline	Well, try as a last resort.	嗯，死馬當活馬醫囉。
Paula	Thanks, anyway.	總之，謝謝妳。
Jacqueline	You are welcome. Good luck!	不客氣，祝妳好運！

實用應答小撇步 2

① rat on me all around / cannot stop bad-mouthing him

到處在打我的小報告／不停地說他的壞話

② I think you did it on purpose / The manager thinks business is business / She thinks what between you two is interminable

我認為你是故意的／主管認為要公事公辦／她認定你們之間沒完沒了

③ This is a very rude(distasteful) behavior / You are such a drama queen / He likes to talk out of thin air

這也太沒水準了吧／你也太沒事找事了吧／他喜歡無中生有

④ becomes the black sheep of the company / be putted on the boss's blacklist / be the boss's favorites

變成公司的害群之馬／被列為主管的黑名單／是老闆眼前的紅人

⑤ What do you suggest me to do? / What else I can do? / Can you suggest me anything to help me?

你建議我怎麼做呢？／我還能做些什麼？／妳能建議我任何事情來幫助我嗎？

⑥ What if she made the same mistake again? / What if he wants to follow his own advice and never listen to anyone? / What if nobody wants to listen to the advices from the manager?

如果她再犯同樣的錯誤了呢？／萬一他想一意孤行呢？／假如沒有人願意聽主管的建議呢？

⑦ I want to speak to your store manager / Please let your boss(manager) come to talk with me / Please ask the person in charge contact me

請你們店長來溝通／請妳的上司來和我談／請負責這件事情的人與我聯繫

💬 單字與句型

1. **do them justice** 替他們主持公道、公平地對待他們
   此片語為 do + someone + justice = do + justice + to + someone。
   Parents should do justice to every child. 父母應當對每個小孩都公平對待。

2. **staff room** 茶水間、員工休息室
   各國對茶水間的定義不同，英語上也有不同說法。在英國有kitchen（可供炊煮）和pantry room（沒有炊煮器具）兩種。在台灣則說成tea room，有些公家單位則是以kitchen作為統一的茶水間英語。一般說staff room，就可以明白了。

3. **take his shift** 幫他代班
   Could you take my shift on Monday? 你週一可以幫我代班嗎？

4. **rat on** 打小報告
   rat就是中文老鼠的意思，英語裡將老鼠作為密告者代表。此為動詞，當名詞使用就是指密告的人。
   She ratted on me, and that's why I lost my job. 她密告我，害我丟掉了工作。

5. **bad-mouth** 說壞話
   Jerry always bad-mouth his manager. 傑瑞總是說他主管的壞話。

6. **personal grudge** 個人恩怨 也可以簡單說成It is personal。

7. **distasteful** *adj.* 沒有水準的（行為），只能拿來形容事、物，不能用來形容人。
   a distasteful joke / book / movie / behavior 一個沒水準的笑話／書籍／電影／行為

8. **drama queen** 沒事找事的人、愛找麻煩的人
   drama是連續劇的意思，此指如連續劇女王般的要處處惹人注意，引申為愛找麻煩、沒事找事做的人。

💬 練習題

- I don't have _____ against John.
- Kelly is the _____ in our office.
- Could you _____ this morning?
- The coffee machine at _____ is broken.

- 我和約翰之間沒有<u>個人恩怨</u>。
- 凱莉是我們辦公室裡<u>大驚小怪</u>的人。
- 妳今天上午可以<u>幫我代班</u>嗎？
- <u>茶水間</u>的咖啡機壞了。

💬 解　答

1. personal grudge
2. drama queen
3. take my shift
4. staff room / tea room / kitchen / pantry room

Unit 04

上司家人抱怨
Boss's Family Complaint

對話 1 Conversation 1

Tracy	Barbara Brown's office. How can I help you?	芭芭拉布朗的辦公室。有什麼可以為您效勞？
Mr. Brown	Please connect me with Barbara. This is her husband.	請幫我接芭芭拉。我是她先生。
Tracy	How are you, Mr. Brown? I am sorry, but she has a guest right now. Would you like to leave a message?	您好嗎，布朗先生？很抱歉，她目前有訪客。您想要留言嗎？
Mr. Brown	No, thanks. Could you possibly ask her to call me back as soon as possible? The kid is in the hospital and she doesn't want to leave the hospital without her mother picking her up!	不用了，謝謝。麻煩你請她盡快回我電話？孩子在醫院，而且沒有她媽媽接的話，她不肯出院。
Tracy	I see, Mr. Brown. I guarantee that Barbara will get this message. [①] Anything else I can do for you?	好的，布朗先生。我保證芭芭拉會收到留言的。還有其他事情我可以幫您的嗎？
Mr. Brown	Yes. My phone is running out	有的。我的手機快沒電

	battery, [2] so ask her to call to the hospital. [3]	了，請她打到醫院來吧。
Tracy	Sure, what's the number, please? [4]	沒問題，請問電話號碼是幾號呢？
Mr. Brown	02-12345678.	02-12345678。
Tracy	OK, I am writing down.	好的，我正在記下來。
Mr. Brown	It's time for getting off work [5] why there are still visitors at your office? She just cannot leave work early! [6]	現在是下班時間，為什麼你們辦公室還有訪客呢？她就是不能早點下班！
Tracy	I am really sorry, Mr. Brown. This appointment has been booked a long time ago. [7] The kid was suddenly sent to the hospital, and she's also very anxious about this.	很抱歉，布朗先生。這個拜訪是很久之前就安排好的，孩子臨時在醫院，她也心急如焚。
Mr. Brown	Is the visitor still there?	那位訪客還在嗎？
Tracy	I am afraid the answer is yes.	恐怕答案是「是的」。
Mr. Brown	All right, all right. I'd better go back to the kid soon.	好了好了，不多說了。我趕緊回到孩子身旁去。
Tracy	Sure. Barbara will make it as soon as possible. Good bye, Mr. Brown.	好的。芭芭拉會盡快趕過去。再見，布朗先生。

實用應答小撇步 1

① I assure you that you will receive the payment / I confirmed that the ship will arrive before 5th, September / She guaranteed that you will receive the products on next Monday

我確保您會收到貨款的／我確認船會在9月5日前抵達／她保證過會讓你們在下週一收到商品

② I got another call / Her cellphone is disabled / There is no money inside my EasyCard

我有電話插播進來／她的手機被停用了／我的悠遊卡裡沒錢了

③ call me at home / send by express mail to the office / delivery to number seventeen branch

打到我家來吧／快遞到公司來吧／寄到17號分店去吧

④ What is the address? / What is the extension(fax) number? / What is your E-Mail address? / What date is the sending(arriving) day?

請問地址是哪裡呢？／請問分機號碼（傳真）是幾號？／請問您的電子郵箱是什麼呢？／請問寄出（抵達）日期是幾號？

⑤ We are not available now / It is a national holiday / Today is Day Off

現在是非上班時間／現在是國定假日／今天是我們的公休日

⑥ He just cannot submit report on time / Can't you just finish your work soon?

他就是無法準時交報告／你就是不能快點完成妳的工作嗎？

⑦ This meeting was confirmed six months(half a year) ago / This order was placed last week / This business trip was agreed two months ago

這個會議是半年前就確定的／這個訂單是上週就下訂的／這趟出差是兩個月前就說好的

對話 **2** Conversation **2**

Henry	Hi, Gordon. How was your exhibition trip last week?	嗨，戈登。上週出國參展還順利吧？
Gordon	It was very good. Thanks for asking.	很好，謝謝關心。
Henry	Did my father demand that you guys should finish a lot of work again?	我老爸是不是又要求你們應該完成很多工作啦？
Gordon	Not really, I think the boss was only try to let us do our best.	不會啦，老闆也是試著讓我們可以把事情做到最好。
Henry	You always kiss my father's ass. ①	你總是拍我爸馬屁。
Gordon	I am telling you the truth.	我說的是真的。
Henry	Whatever. Not afraid to let you know that he's also an overly demanding father, asking us to do this and that. Each of us cannot take his harshness.	都可以啦。不怕你知道，他在家也是很兇的，要求這個、要求那個。我們每個人都受不了他的嚴厲。
Gordon	Maybe you can think it from another perspective. Just try to think things from a different angle, for example, what if I met his expectations. ②	或許換個角度想就好了。你可以試試看從另一個角度想事情，譬如說，如果我達到他的期望的話。

Henry	No way! ③ Nobody can meet his requirements.	不可能的啦！沒人可以做到他的要求。
Gordon	Well, it's hard to say. His secretary, Christine, is doing great and boss always praise her. ④	這很難說唷。他的秘書克莉絲汀就很厲害，老闆經常誇獎她呢。
Henry	I have never heard of such a thing. ⑤	這我可從來沒聽說過。
Gordon	Maybe you haven't stayed with this company long enough.	或許你在公司的時間還不夠久。
Henry	Whatever you say. Right, could you help write the conference record for me?	隨便啦。對了，這次的會議紀錄可不可以麻煩你幫我寫？
Gordon	I don't think so, Henry, I didn't attend the meeting.	不可能吧，亨利，我又沒有去參加會議。
Henry	Just write it in a perfunctory manner.	隨便寫寫交差就得了吧。
Gordon	No wonder the boss scolds you all the time. ⑥ Don't say that I didn't warm you, this kind attitude could get you being told off wherever you go.	難怪老闆會罵你！別說我沒有警告你，這種態度到哪裡都會挨罵。⑦
Henry	All right, all right. I will do it myself.	好吧，自己寫就自己寫。
Gordon	You should take your work seriously.	你應該要認真對待你的工作才行啊。

實用應答小撇步 2

① The manager of the sales department is always talking people's head off / She always picks the easier tasks to do / He's always late

業務部主管總是喋喋不休／她總是撿輕鬆的工作做／他老是遲到

② You can try to rewrite the proposal / I can repeat that / He could rearrange the meeting for next week

你可以試著重寫提案／我可以重講一次／他可以下週再排一次會議

③ Stop dreaming / A leopard doesn't (cannot / never) change its spots / Over my dead body (You are dreaming)!

別做夢了啦／牛牽到北京還是牛／除非我死了，否則休想（你在作夢）！

④ The President usually speaks in praise of him / The client complains her

sometimes / The consumers often returned purchase this month

董事長經常表揚他／客戶有時會抱怨她／消費者這個月經常退貨

⑤ We never heard of this before / She has never said anything like this before / We have never agreed this thing

我們從來沒聽過這件事／她從沒說過這樣的話／我們從來沒有同意過這件事情

⑥ No wonder you are getting fired / No wonder she doesn't receive any favor from her boss / No wonder the shipment is delayed

難怪你會被炒魷魚／難怪她不受她的主管寵愛／難怪貨物延遲了

⑦ It is unacceptable with this kind of saying wherever you go / This kind of answer will be accepted nowhere / The explanation like this is not welcome anywhere

這種說詞到哪裡都不會被接受／這樣的回答到哪裡都行不通／這樣的解釋到哪裡都不會受歡迎

💬 單字與句型

1. get off work = leave work　下班
2. appointment *n.*　拜訪行程
   也有約會、任命的意思。

   appointment to the general manager　被任命為總經理

   book(cancel) an appointment　訂（取消）一個預約（約會）
3. Day Off　公休日
   關於假日有幾種說法：國定假日（法定的休假日），例如：元旦、農曆新年、228紀念日……等等，英文稱作National Holidays、Legal Holidays、Official Holidays、Public Holidays。另一種是該領域的人放的假日，例如：勞工節(Labor Day)、護士節(Nurse Day)、軍人節(Armed Forces Day)，英文稱作national public holidays。
4. order was placed　訂單被下訂了
   原為place an order（下訂單），此為倒裝句。

   I already placed an order for ten thousands of women shirts.　我已經下訂了一萬件女性襯衫。
5. kiss someone's ass　拍某人馬屁
   ass也可以用butt（臀部）取代。
6. perspective *n.*　觀點
   換個角度思考還可以寫成think differently、think it from another (a different) angle。
7. in a perfunctory manner　敷衍了事地、馬虎地
   perfunctory本身是形容詞，敷衍的意思，此句作為副詞修飾前面的動詞。
8. talking someone's head off　喋喋不休
   原意是講話講到某人的頭都要掉了。也可以寫成talking someone's ear off。
9. A leopard doesn't change its spots　牛牽到北京還是牛
   原意是豹難以改變牠身上的花紋，引申為指人江山易改，本性難移。

練習題

- kiss someone's butt
- A leopard doesn't change its spots
- in a perfunctory manner
- talking someone's head off

- 喋喋不休
- 打馬虎眼
- 拍馬屁
- 江山易改，本性難移

解　答

依照英語的順序

1. 拍馬屁
2. 江山易改，本性難移
3. 打馬虎眼
4. 喋喋不休

主題 ② 抱怨處理 Deal With Complaints

職場補給站：處理抱怨的5大黃金步驟

　　曾經有統計顯示，如果一位消費者對於某家店有好感，他／她會告訴7個朋友；相反的，如果曾經受氣於某家店，他／她會告訴12個朋友！這個數字告訴我們處理和解決抱怨的重要性。

　　抱怨有可能來自外部（客人），也有可能產生自內部（員工）；所謂「有滿意的員工，才有滿意的顧客」，處理員工的情緒，讓他們對公司的制度可以產生建議或建言，遠比壓抑而最後導致員工抱怨，要來得正面許多。

　　身為職場人，每天都可能接到抱怨的電話、信件，甚至自同事的抱怨，如何第一時間就化解這些情緒，不讓後續醞釀產生更大的衝擊，是很重要的。以下就提供處理抱怨的五大黃金步驟：

❶ 仔細聆聽，先讓對方說完(Listen carefully and let them finish first)。你我可能遇過正在生氣想要抒發情緒上的時候，都不喜歡被人家打斷；所以遇到抱怨，第一件事情就是讓對方先把不滿的情緒宣洩完畢。

❷ 感同身受(Put yourself in their shoes)。置身處地為他人設想很重要，很多衝突的產生就是因為認為「這件事對我來說沒有很重要」，卻忽略了別人對「這件事」的重視程度，輕率地處理也就導致了對方的不滿。舉例來說：到中式餐館吃飯，菜都上齊了卻遲遲等不到飯上來，就會讓客人無法開動；如果請客人「先吃菜不就好了？」，那麼客訴也就跟著來了。

❸ 道歉卻不找理由責怪(Apologize without blaming)。誠摯地道歉即可，不要為事情找藉口，或者責怪對方、同事、甚至公司。如此一來，比較容易營造和緩的氣氛；而不是延伸出更多的抱怨，也不會讓對方找到繼續抱怨的理由。

❹ 問對方可以接受的解決方案(Asking "What would be an acceptable solution to you?")。一味地抱怨是沒有用的，有禮貌地詢問對方，他／她心目中理想的解決方案是什麼？這一招不論是面對顧客、客戶、甚至同事都一樣有效，畢竟事情已經發生，找到解決方法才是重新獲得人心的妙招。

❺ 解決問題，或者盡快找到可以解決的人來(Solve the problem, or quickly find someone who can solve it)。如果你自己就可以和對方討論出解決的方案，那麼恭喜你，抱怨被順利處理了；萬一自己無法處理時，告訴對方，你將會找誰來處理，把你的或者對方的（事前或者事後要通知這個負責人）聯繫方式告訴抱怨的人，然後提供一個期限（例如：明天下午五點前、某月某日）來做進度追蹤。

　　雖然有時候，抱怨只是情緒的抒發，如果認真聽完，對方可能也不會有進一步要求。但是如果處理的人給予後續的進度報告，通常會獲得抱怨的一方良善的回應，甚至從此成為公司死忠的客人／員工。所謂「一念天堂、一念地獄(The mind is its own place and in itself, can make a Heaven of Hell, a Hell of Heaven.)」，被慎重對待的抱怨，最終也會獲得慎重的回饋（品牌忠誠／員工忠誠）。

Part
Three

公司導覽
A Company Tour

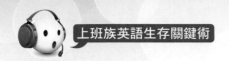

Unit 01 介紹公司歷史和特色 Introducing Company History and Features

對話 1 Conversation 1

Ken　Hey, Daisy. I am nervous about the client visiting tomorrow.

嗨，黛西。明天客戶要來，我好緊張喔。

Daisy　What are you nervous about?

你在緊張什麼？

Ken　My boss asked me to introduce the company's background to them.

主管要我介紹公司背景給客戶知道。

Daisy　I think it's a piece of cake to you.

對你來說很容易啊。

Ken　It's not. I only know that the company was founded in 2005, ① as now, the company has 300 full-time employees. ② Here is where headquarter is located and there is a factory in China. ③ That's all.

才不呢。我只知道公司成立於2005年，目前全職員工300人。這裡是總公司，還有一個工廠在大陸，就這樣。

Daisy　You can add some historical stories, or our company's mission or vision, so it won't be so boring.

你可以添加一些歷史故事，或者我們的理念，聽起來才不會無聊。

Ken　Such as?

例如說呢？

Daisy　For example, the story of our founder started from scratch or the

像是創辦人白手起家的故事啦，經過金融風暴，現

82

	current chairman not only stabilized the business, but also expands to more countries despite the global financial crisis. Moreover, the company's vision is letting more consumers enjoy better quality products.[4]	任董事長除了穩住公司生意，還拓展到更多國家。以及公司的理念就是希望讓更多消費者享受到更優質的產品……等等。
Ken	Are you sure that the clients will like to hear these?	你確定客戶們會有興趣聽這些？
Daisy	Do you have a better idea?[5]	不然你有更好的想法嗎？
Ken	Well, I am not sure. It just sounds very unrealistic.[6]	嗯，我也不知道。這聽起來很不實際。
Daisy	I think it would be sound much more vividly if you add some stories, rather than just talking those backgrounds.	我只是覺得在公司背景以外，添加些小故事會更生動。
Ken	Why don't you help me to write the draft, and I buy you a lunch.	不如你幫我寫草稿吧？我請你吃午餐。
Daisy	In your dreams! I have plenty of things on my hands.	想得美！我手上有一大堆事情呢。
Ken	It seems that I have to work late at night.	看來我又要加班熬夜了。
Daisy	Carry on that.	加油。

實用應答小撇步　1

① Since its inception, we have more than one million employees / We have more than three thousand suppliers (vendors, third party) / In terms of patent application numbers, our company occupies a leading position in Taiwan

成立至今，已經有超過100萬員工／合作廠商超過3千個 ／我司在專利申請數量上，在台灣佔據領導地位

② Company founder's wish is to provide consumers chemical-free skin care products / Our ideal is to achieve 20% energy savings of the world every year

公司創辦人的想法是希望提供消費者不含化學原料的保養品／我司的理想就是要讓世界能源每年節省20%以上

③ I have a better proposal / Do you have a better solution? / What's on his mind?

我有更好的提案／你有更好的解決方法嗎？／他有什麼主意？

④ This thing sounds unbelievable(incredible) / David seems finished (gone) / You seem screwed up

這件事聽起來很不可思議／大衛看起來是玩完了（完蛋了）／你似乎是搞砸了

⑤ I have a bunch of bills this month / You have a plenty of projects that haven't been finished / He has many fair-weather friends / She has a lot of cosmetics in her bag

我這個月有一大堆帳單呢／你有一堆計畫案還沒有完成呢／他有一群酒肉朋友 ／她的包包裡有一大堆化妝品

對話 **2** Conversation **2**

	(At Meeting Room)	(在會議室裡)
Brad	We are happy to have you visit, Mr. Duke Warwick.	很高興您的到來，杜克華威先生。
Duke	Please, just call me Duke.	叫我杜克吧。
Brad	No problem. There still are few minutes before the meeting, let me show you our showroom now.	好的。離會議還有幾分鐘，我先帶您逛逛我們公司的展覽室吧。
Duke	OK, I am looking forward to it. ①	我很期待呢。
Brad	Now, as you see it, here shows the history of our company and precious documents. ②	如您所見，這裡展示了我們公司的歷史，以及一些珍貴資料。
Duke	I can see that your company has kept historical materials well from these photos on the wall.	我可以從牆上的照片看出來貴公司將歷史資料保存得很好。
Brad	Yes, the general manager is a nostalgic person and this company was founded by his father. ③	是的。我們總經理是一個相當念舊的人，這間公司是他的父親創立的。
Duke	I see. ④ What does it show on this picture?	原來如此。這張照片是什麼意思呢？
Brad	That's our staff came spontaneously to help as well as giving donation to The 921 Earthquake.	是921大地震後，我們公司員工自發地到現場幫忙，還有送上捐款的照片。

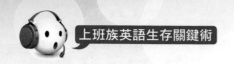
Duke	It's really impressive. ⑤	真令人感動。
Brad	This photo shows our general manager met the President at the year we won the National Quality Award. ⑥	這張是總統接見公司總經理的照片。那一年我們獲得了國家品質獎。
Duke	Which means the quality of the product is trustworthy.	那表示貴公司的產品品質應該是值得信賴的。
Brad	You can rest assured. ⑦	這個您可以放心！
Duke	I would like to go to men's room before the meeting starts.	我想在會議開始前先去一趟洗手間。
Brad	Sure. Just go straight on and turn left. ⑧	沒問題。直走左轉就是了。
Duke	Thanks. See you later.	謝謝你。等會見。

實用應答小撇步 2

① I am surprised / I am impressed / I am waiting for your reply (response, feedback) / I am all ears

我很驚訝／真是令我印象深刻／我正在等待您的回信（回覆、回饋）／我洗耳恭聽

② This slide shows the very first look of our company's headquarter(factory) / The four founders of our company are on the photo / What you see here are the displays of our product over these years

這張投影片顯示了我們最初公司總部（工廠）的樣子／這張照片上有我們四位創辦人的合影／現在您看到的是我們歷年產品的展示

③ The (ex)chairman is a public-spirited man / We are a company which treats employees as families / Company executives are the people who come from all areas and do well above average

我們的（前）董事長是一位熱心公益的人／我們是一間將員工視作是家人的公司／公司高層都是各領域的佼佼者

④ So that's how it is / I don't think so / Now I understood why / He suddenly realized that...

原來如此／我不認為如此／終於知道為什麼了／他恍然大悟原來…

⑤ I am impressed / I am touched(moved) by this movie

真令我印象深刻／我被這部電影感動了

⑥ This year, we doubled our sales / The competitor dominated the market last year / We go public this year

這一年我們業績成長兩倍／去年競爭對手的市佔率遙遙領先／今年我們公司股票上市了

⑦ Just relax / Now, breathe easy! / Don't worry about it / You can trust(count on) me　放心吧／放心啦！／別擔心／你可以信任我

⑧ go down the hall / walk straight to the end / turn right and you will see it on your left hand side　直走到底／直走到底／右轉後就在左手邊

單字與句型

1. headquarter *n.* 總部、總公司
   分公司是branch，原意是樹的分支。

2. company's mission or vision 公司的任務或願景
   公司願景屬於未來的規劃，通常是一個理想的境界；而任務則是指為了達成
   願景所要做的事情。

3. global financial crisis 全球金融風暴
   也可以寫作economic crisis（經濟危機/風暴）。另外幾個和經濟有關的英
   文有：

   economic downturn / recession / slump 經濟衰退

   economic depression 經濟蕭條

   economic upswing 經濟復甦

   economic growth 經濟成長

4. inception *n.* 成立以來、創建以來

5. patent application 專利申請
   此作名詞使用，申請專利寫作apply patent。

6. fair-weather friend 酒肉朋友
   照原意翻譯，就是好天氣的朋友，表示只有在好天氣才陪你出門，壞天氣就
   不理你的朋友；引申的意思就是指的是酒肉朋友，只能享樂卻不能同甘。

7. nostalgic *adj.* 懷舊的、念舊的
   nostalgia （名詞）就是念舊、懷舊的意思。在女神卡卡（Lady Gaga）的
   掌聲（Applause）這首歌裡，就有一句 "Nostalgia's for geeks"（怪胎
   才會懷舊呢）的歌詞。

8. public-spirited 熱心公益的

💬 練習題

Please write down the contrary terms.

請寫下相反詞。

- branch → _____
- economic upswing → _____
- eager for quick success and instant benefit → _____
- trendy → _____

- 分公司 → 總公司（總部）
- 經濟復甦 → 經濟衰退
- 急功近利的 → 熱心公益的
- 新潮的 → 懷舊的

💬 解 答

1. headquarter
2. economic downturn / recession / slump
3. public-spirited
4. nostalgic

Unit 02 介紹公司部門與產品 Introducing Departments and Products

對話 1 Conversation 1

Eva	Hi, Pearce. May I have few minutes of your time? [1]	嗨，皮爾斯，可以耽誤您幾分鐘時間嗎？
Pearce	Sure, no problem. What is it?	當然，沒問題。什麼事？
Eva	I would like to confirm with you the new version of company department and product introduction. [2]	我想和您確認一下公司新版的部門與產品簡介。
Pearce	You have done the writing?	妳寫好了？
Eva	Yes.	是的。
Pearce	Great. Let's go through it together.	太好了。我們一起來過一遍吧。
Eva	Well, our company adopts flat organization structure. [3] There are four departments right now, they are Producing Department, Administration Department, Marketing and Sales Department.	嗯，我們公司實行扁平化組織。目前僅有4個部門，分別是生產部、行政部、行銷部與業務部。
Pearce	Very good, go on, please.	很好，繼續。
Eva	Our company is also certified to an ISO standard. [4]	公司也榮獲ISO認證。

Pearce	You should say what products we have; then, introduce what producing certificates we won.	應該先説有什麼產品，再説產品獲得了哪些認證。
Eva	Sure. We produce cooking oils such as peanut oil, olive oil and sunflower oil.	好的。我們公司生產食用油，例如：花生油、橄欖油、葵花油。
Pearce	Add "world-class quality", and "we holds the number one market share in Taiwan." ⑤	加上一句「世界級品質」，以及我們的「市場佔有率是台灣第一名」。
Eva	Will do. We are also the sole agent of Italian Olive oil, and we wish to provide our customers more choices through this. ⑥	知道了。我司也獨家代理來自義大利的橄欖油，希望藉此提供台灣消費者更多的選擇。
Pearce	I think here we use "We wish to provide Taiwanese consumers better choices" will sound better.	我覺得這裡用「希望提供台灣消費者更好的選擇」聽起來更貼切一點。
Eva	OK, no problem.	好的，沒問題。
Pearce	Last thing, please add our annual revenue is more than NTD$ 1 billion.	最後再補上我們的年營業額超過新台幣10億元，就完成了。
Eva	Sure. I will E-Mail you when I finish modification.	好的。我修改好後會再E-Mail給您。
Pearce	Great. Try to provide before this Friday. ⑦	好的，盡量在這個週五以前提供。

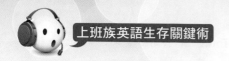
實用應答小撇步 1

① Excuse me for a second / Do you have a minute? / Sorry for disturbing (to interrupt)

抱歉打擾一下／您有時間嗎？／抱歉打斷一下

② I reconfirmed (confirmed again) / This has not yet been confirmed / Did you confirm this with your manager?

我再次確認過了／這件事還有待確認／妳和主管確認過了嗎？

③ Our company is a streamlining organization / Our General Manager has full responsibility for all facets of the company / Their company adopts a top-down leadership style

我們公司組織很精簡／我們是總經理制／他們公司是從上而下的領導管理風格

④ The company got several food safety certifications / The factory won many public safety awards

公司榮獲多項食品安全認證／工廠榮獲多項公共安全大獎

⑤ The industry's the most complete line of juice products/ The importing(exporting) items are the most various / Brand awareness is the highest in the world

果汁生產線是業界最齊全／進（出）口品項是台灣最多樣／品牌知名度是世界最高

⑥ One of the dealers(distributors) of Swiss chocolate / Sole distributor of Canadian kids clothing / Agent(broker) of Japanese singers

瑞士巧克力的經銷商之一／加拿大兒童服裝的總經銷／日本歌星的經紀人

⑦ It's better if you can finish it before the 1st of next month / No later than next Wednesday / Please provide me details as soon as possible

最好在下個月一日前完成／最遲不要超過下周三／盡快提供我細節

對話 2 | Conversation 2

Felicia	Hi, Urania. I appreciate your coming for interviewing today.	嗨，尤瑞妮亞。歡迎妳今天來到我們公司進行採訪。
Urania	Thank you for being willing to be interviewed. I haven't seen you since last new product launch.	也謝謝妳願意接受採訪。上次新品發表會後就沒見過妳了。
Felicia	Yes, I think that was six months ago. So, what do we talk about today?	對呀，有半年了。那麼我們今天從何談起呢？
Urania	I would like to know that your company is going to launch new products in the near future?	我想知道公司未來還有新產品推出嗎？
Felicia	Yes, we are. But the time hasn't come yet.	會有的，但是公布的時機點還沒有到。
Urania	A new generation mobile phone? What's new feature will be added?	新一代手機？會有什麼新增加的功能呢？
Felicia	It's confidential. [①] The concept is from military equipment. [②]	請容我保密。但是概念來自軍用設備。
Urania	WOW, how exciting! Your R&D department is full of imagination.	哇，多令人興奮啊！研發部門真是想像力豐富。
Felicia	This is the research achievement of Marketing and R&D Department. [③]	這是行銷部門與研發部門共同研究的成果。

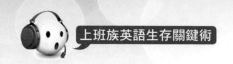

Urania	I heard that the company is restructuring? ④	還有我聽說公司要重整？
Felicia	Well, that's right. To meet new challenges, we are going to separate Sales team into two teams which are For Consumer and For Dealers.	嗯，是的。為了因應新的挑戰，我們打算將業務部門拆成對消費者以及對經銷商的兩個團隊。
Urania	Is this because of the decline of performance in the first half? ⑤	是因為上半年業績下滑的關係嗎？
Felicia	Of course not. This is for providing a better service to our customers. ⑥	當然不是。是為了給我們的客戶更好的服務。
Urania	Right, I will write these down, however, I will add my opinion at the same time.	好吧，這些我會寫下來，但是我也會加入我的看法。
Felicia	Sure. Please give us as much positive reviews as you can.	當然，請對我們盡量維持正面評語。
Urania	No problem. So, I should be leaving now.	客氣了。那我先離開了。
Felicia	Let me walk you to the door. ⑦	讓我送妳到門口吧。

實用應答小撇步 2

① Please don't spill the beans / Don't let the cat out of the bag / Just between you and me

請保密（勿洩漏）

② It's ergonomic design / It' inspired by nature

設計符合人體工學／靈感來自大自然

③ It's the effort of sales staff's hard working for the last six months / It's the results of cooperation between the firm and the dealers / It's the result of satisfying consumers

是業務同仁努力半年的成果／是公司與經銷商合作的結果／是滿足消費者的結果

④ reengineering the organization / reelection the board / The store is going to reopen

組織要重組／董事會要改選／這家店準備要新開張

⑤ sales revenues increased last month / Last season's shipments decline sharply / The number of VIP reduced five percent last year

上個月營業額上升了／上一季出貨量銳減／去年VIP人數減少了5%

⑥ To give more profit to downstream firms / Providing consumers more choice / Providing hotel customers a better holiday (vacation)

給下游廠商更多的利潤／給消費者更多的選擇／給房客更優質的假期

⑦ Let him take you downstairs / Let me walk you to lane entrance / Can you walk yourself to the door?

讓他送你到樓下吧／讓我送妳到巷口吧／你可以自己走到門口嗎？

單字與句型

1. go through　很快地瀏覽一遍
   這個單詞還有以下的意思。

   Please don't go through my stuff.　請不要任意亂翻我的東西。

   My son goes through his shoes pretty a season.　我兒子每季的鞋子汰舊換新地很快。

2. certified *adj.*　合法的、認証的

3. modification *n.*　修改
   此為名詞，動詞為modify。

4. top-down　由上而下的
   反義詞則寫作bottom-up，由下而上的。

5. various *adj.*　多樣的、不同的、各式各樣的
   For various reasons the company needs to downsize.　因為種種原因，公司必須精簡組織。

6. new product launch　新品發表會
   發佈新產品的動詞就是用launch。

   We are going to launch a brand new cell phone next month.　下個月我們即將發表一款新手機。

7. in the near future　未來、將來
   要注意的是，也有英文學者批評此語是贅語，可以直接説soon（即將、快了）即可。

8. restructure　重整、重組
   同義詞還有reorganization。

9. R&D department　研發部門

10. ergonomic　符合人體工學的

11. downstream firms　下游廠商
    上游廠商寫作upstream firms(companies)。

💬 練習題

Please write down the contrary terms.

請寫下相反詞。

- I am going to attend a _____ next Monday.
- This chair is _____ .
- She is the spokesman of _____.
- For _____ reasons he retailed early.
- The _____ of this certification is totally _____ .

- 下周一我要參加一場新品發表會。
- 這是一張符合人體工學設計的椅子。
- 她是研發部門與行政管理部門的發言人。
- 因為種種原因，他提前退休。
- 這張證書的修改是完全合法的。

💬 解　答

1. new product launch
2. ergonomic design
3. R&D department
4. various
5. modification, certified

Unit 03 介紹公司部門與幹部 Introducing Departments and Staff

對話 1 Conversation 1

Charlie	You are Terry who reports for duty today.	你是今天報到的泰瑞吧。
Terry	Yes, this is me.	你好，我是。
Charlie	You can call me Charlie. I am the human resources coordinator. ①	你可以叫我查理。我是人力資源部門的專員。
Terry	Hi, Charlie.	嗨，查理。
Charlie	I'll give you a tour of Departments and their Managers today.	今天我帶你認識公司部門和主管們。
Terry	Great! Where should we start?	太好了！我們從哪裡開始？
Charlie	Let's start with your department. The manager is David, but he rarely comes to office. ② You mainly report to the Assistant Manager, Kin.	就從你們部門開始吧。你的主管是大衛，平時他很少進公司。你主要回報給副理，金。
Terry	OK, no problem.	好的，沒問題。
Charlie	Retail Department is right next to your Department, mainly takes	你們部門旁邊就是零售業務部門，主要負責和零售

	responsible for communicating with retail stores about how to sell our products. Their manager is Lee, take care of him, he bites. [3][4]	賣場溝通如何銷售我們的產品。主管是李,他不是個好惹的人物。
Terry	Got you, I will be careful.	知道了,我會小心。
Charlie	Let' go upstairs. Here you see is Accounting Department, all beauties. Their manager is Ann, she is very cautious, any documents to her needs to be confirmed again and again. [5]	我們上樓吧。這裡是會計部,都是美女們。她們的主管是安,她很謹慎,任何給她的資料你自己都要確認再三。
Terry	I'll remember that.	我會記得的。
Charlie	Legal Department is at the same floor with Accounting Department, right here. [6] The manager is Bob who wears glasses, he also pays a lot of attention on word choice. But don't worry, his assistant, Sally, usually fixes for us.	法務部和會計部同層樓,就在這裡。主管是戴眼鏡的鮑勃,他也很計較用字遣詞,不過別擔心,他的副手莎莉,通常會幫忙我們修改。
Terry	Which one is Sally?	哪位是莎莉呢?
Charlie	She is out for lunch. She's the short girl who usually ties ponytail. [7]	她去吃午飯了吧,不在座位上,就是經常綁馬尾的小個子女生。
Terry	OK, I memorized them all.	好的,我都記住了。
Charlie	Then wish you a nice first working day.	那就祝你上班第一天愉快囉。

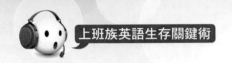

實用應答小撇步 1

① She is an Account Executive of PR company / I am the Team Leader(Manager) of this restaurant / He is Technician(Engineer) of IT Department

她是公關公司的專案執行／我是這間餐廳的領班（店長）／他是資訊部門的技術員（工程師）

② General Manager is usually on a business trip for multinational meetings / My supervisor always attends a lot of seminars / Sales Representatives not often go to visit customers

總經理經常出差參加跨國會議／我的主管總是要參加很多研討會／銷售代表們不太常去拜訪客戶

③ be responsible for dealing with Government Offices / take responsible for public relations communicating with stockholders / be responsible for business development in Greater China

負責和政府機關打交道／負責對股東們的公關溝通／負責大中華區的業務開發

④ She is hard / Most of the time, he is sweet / My supervisor is unreasonable / The clients usually roar at me

她很兇／他大多數時候很體貼／我的主管不明事理／客戶經常對我咆哮

⑤ He always does gingerly / She is always careless

他總是小心翼翼／她老是粗心

⑥ The company and suppliers are located at the same country / Our customers are mostly at South America / Sara is sitting right next to me

公司和供應商都在同一個縣市／我們客戶多半在南美洲／我和莎拉的位子就在隔壁

⑦ He is the one who wears a mustache and with punch belly / She is the one who wears eye shadow(blush) / The one who wears curls(wavy hair)

他是留鬍子、肚子微凸的那位／她是畫了眼影（腮紅）的那位／就是捲髮（直髮）的那位

對話 2 Conversation 2

Libby	Sorry, Enlyn. May I bother you for a second?	抱歉，艾姆林。可以打擾你一下嗎？
Emlyn	Hi, Libby. What's the matter?	嗨，莉比。怎麼了？
Libby	Nothing important. It's just I am new and occasionally come to meeting at head office, so I want to clarify few things about the Departments and who are responsible for what matters.	沒什麼重要的。只是我剛進公司又偶而才來總公司開會，有幾個部門和同仁負責的事項想釐清一下。
Emlyn	Sure, no problem. Just shoot.	哦，沒問題呀。盡管問吧。
Libby	Which department has responsibility for the procurement of all goods? [1]	現在商品的進貨是哪個部門負責？
Emlyn	That would be the Purchasing Department. The supervisor is May.	現在由採購部門負責。主管是梅。
Libby	Wasn't she responsible for Accounting Department?	她不是原來負責會計部？
Emlyn	Yes, that's why the Accounting Department is looking for successors of May's position. [2]	是呀。會計部現在正在找人接梅的位置呢。
Libby	There are also some changes in	人事部好像也有一些變

	Human Resources Department? ③	動？
Emlyn	Only Amber took maternity leave, and Jack is now doing her work temporarily. ④	只有安柏休產假，由傑克暫代她的工作罷了。
Libby	OK, so I am wrong.	哦，那是我記錯了。
Emlyn	Maybe you are talking about Planning Department? They always have a high turnover rate. ⑤	你說的是企劃部門吧？他們這個部門一向流動率很高。
Libby	Yes, and it's quite annoying when memorizing new colleagues.	是呀，每次要記新來的同事，真的很麻煩。
Emlyn	Anything else?	還有呢？
Libby	That's all.	就這樣了吧。
Emlyn	Oh, right, I forgot to tell you that they changed spokesman. Assistant General Manager is now concurrently serving as company's spokesman. ⑥	哦，對了。忘記告訴妳，發言人換人了。現在由副總經理兼任。
Libby	Hope they can find the successor soon, or he will spread himself too thin. ⑦	希望他們盡快找到繼任人選，否則副總恐怕要分身乏術了。

實用應答小撇步 2

① Which department is responsible for this promotion event? / Which restaurant is taking responsible for catering at noon? / Which customs broker is responsible for customs?

這次促銷活動是哪個部門負責的？／中午的外燴是哪家餐廳負責的？／報關是哪個報關行負責的？

② He is looking for new employees / We are long for partners / The firm is going to add some security guards

他正在找新的員工／我們正在找合夥人／公司將增聘警衛人手

③ There will be a major personnel change in Financial Department / There will be half of the Legal Department employees fired / We have stable workforce recently

財務部將有一個人事大變動／法務部將裁撤一半的人力／公司人事近來很穩定

④ I am temporarily taking the position as a department supervisor / He takes his colleague's shift today

我暫時接替部門主管的工作／他今天幫同事代班

⑤ The company always replaces the old products by new very quick / This restaurant has a high table turnover rate

公司產品一向汰舊換新很快／這家餐廳翻桌率很高

⑥ We found a new candidate / This position is empty for a long time

我們找到新的人選了／這個職位空著很久了

⑦ You can multi-task / You should try to zero task a little bit

你可以一人當多人用，處理多重事務／妳應該試著放慢工作步調

單字與句型

1. report for duty　報到
   同義詞還有on board，多用在工作上；check-in，多用在登機、住宿登記的時候。

   Today is my first day on board.　今天是我報到的第一天。

2. word choice　用字遣詞

3. seminar　研討會

4. roar *v.*　咆哮
   電影「Ted」（中文名稱「熊麻吉」）裡有一段歌，就用了thunder，並且形容了它的咆哮聲音。歌詞是：You can't get me, thunder, cause your just God's fart.（你嚇不到我的，閃電，因為你只是上帝放的屁而已。）。

5. wear a mustache　留鬍子
   不同鬍子有不同說法。

   a cookie-brusher，留在上唇的小鬍子。

   Fu Man-Chu，清朝流行的胡滿州鬍（八字鬍）。

   a handlebar mustache，翹鬍子。

   goatee，山羊鬍。

   stubs (bristles) / thorn bush，剛長出來的鬍鬚根。

6. turnover *n.*　進出、周轉
   turnover rate，可以拿來指員工的流動率，也可以指餐廳的翻桌率（客人進出、流動的比率）。

7. spread himself too thin　分身乏術
   原意是把奶油塗抹得太薄了，延伸指一個人放了很多精力在不同事情上。

8. customs *n.*　報關作業、海關
   也有風俗、習俗的意思。

   He is a customs officer.　他是一位海關人員。

   So many countries, so many customs.　各國風俗不盡相同。

練習題

- Restaurants should pursue a _____ .
- She is an excellent _____ .
- I _____ recently.
- He wears _____ .

- 餐廳應該追求高的翻桌率。
- 她是一位優秀的海關人員。
- 我最近分身乏術。
- 他留著山羊鬍子。

解　答

1. high turnover rate
2. customs officer
3. spread myself too thin
4. goatee

主題 ③ 公司導覽 A Company Tour

職場補給站：另類導遊

　　相信大多數人都有參加旅行團的經驗，不管是三五好友一起出國，還是跟著親戚、鄰里遊玩台灣；團裡總是會有一位經驗老到、說學逗唱拿手的人物，我們稱他／她為「導遊」。導遊的工作就是導覽遊玩地的歷史、風景特色，解答團裡的人對於周遭景物的疑問；甚至連「廁所在哪裡？(Where is the restroom please?)」這類的問題，都被期待要解說詳盡。導遊的代價除了每天的導遊費用以外，就屬看到整團的人玩得盡興，以及安全出門、平安回家。

　　隨著全球化商業的到來，國與國之間貿易、溝通的頻繁，應該很少上班族沒有見過客戶到公司裡面來的經驗。既然客戶來到了公司拜訪，總要有個「導遊」來接待吧；從幾點、如何到公司，到蒞臨公司後的行程安排，要見什麼人、要聽什麼簡報、要參觀哪些設備，結束後該怎麼離開，是不是要安排飯局……等等，甚至「公司的洗手間在哪裡、怎麼去？」類似的問題，也得要事先在腦海裡演練一遍，務求以最簡潔的說法讓對方聽懂。

通常在做公司簡介時，會涵蓋以下幾點：

❶ 公司的背景資料(Company history)。成立時間、成立地點、創辦的理由、公司的願景、創辦人的理念……等等。這部分屬於比較制式的部分，只要記得應該要和公司網站上公布的資料一致即可；因為有些客戶，可是會事先上網作功課的。

❷ 目前的發展現況以及未來發展(The Current Development and Future Perspectives)。公司現在的規模、人數、生產線多寡、生產／接單能力，未來準備發展哪些事業／事務……等等。雖然也是屬於制式化的部分，但

是可以視來訪的客戶屬性，以及公司的文化，在這個部分添加一些如何突破困境，達到現在的規模，或者曾經遇到經營問題，但是克服了…等等軟性的說法，會讓人覺得這家公司是有「人性(humanity)」，並且對問題有解決能力的，藉此加深客戶對公司的好印象。

❸ 產品或服務特色(The product or service features)。這個部分也可以視情況用不同的介紹方式，如果是年輕、有活力的公司，也不介意現在示範產品如何使用，甚至搭配背景音樂(background music)，或者展示一段影片等等。

❹ 選一位適合的人來介紹(choose the right person)。既然是對公司以外的人來做簡介，對象是誰，就要找適當的人、用適當的語氣來表達，不但可以順利傳遞公司應該有的形象，對來訪者來說也不會顯得太突兀。舉例來說：牛奶工廠對國外投資者來訪，以及對隔壁幼稚園小朋友的來訪參觀，就應該是由不同特質的人來擔任公司的「導遊(tour guide)」。

❺ 勤加模擬練習(practice, practice and practice)。在訪客來訪之前，通常會視對簡報內容掌握的熟悉程度、對方的層級、來訪的目的不同，而進行適當的模擬演練。有些公司介紹的工作，甚至在半年前展開資料蒐集、現場演練，務必求臨場的那一刻順利與完美。

❻ 勿忘Q&A(do not forget the importance of Q&A)。有些客戶在聽完公司簡介後，會提問，而且問題各式各樣，有些也不一定涵蓋在簡報中，但是客戶就是問了。這時候該怎麼辦？通常針對對方來訪的重要性，最好事先指派當天負責回答的人，或者臨場反應，力求當場解決對方疑問，忌諱讓對方留下疑問離開，因為如此一來，就會影響對方對公司的評價。這也呼應上方提到的模擬練習，惟有準備才是最好的防備。

　　最後，雖然這位另類的導遊可能沒有來自訪客給的「帶團小費(tips)」，但是成功將公司形象傳遞給對方，就是他們最大的收穫。

Part
Four

工廠導覽
A Factory Tour

Unit 01 介紹工廠生產線
Introducing Production Lines

對話 1 Conversation 1

Louis	Hi, Sophia. Welcome to our factory again.	嗨，蘇菲亞。歡迎妳再次到我們工廠來參觀。
Sophia	It has been a long time. I think it was ten years ago when I visited here.	好久不見。上次我來是十年前了。
Louis	Time flies.	時光飛逝呢。
Sophia	Indeed.	對呀。
Louis	Let me show you the production line, this is what so called "Money Making Machine." [①]	我先帶妳參觀生產線吧，這可是我們工廠的「印鈔機」。
Sophia	How's that?	怎麼說呢？
Louis	You can see the products come out one by one, doesn't it look like printing money? If we can sell them all, the company will make big money.	產品一個個出來，不就像印鈔票一樣嗎？全賣掉的話，公司就賺錢啦。
Sophia	Very nice description.	形容得真好。

Louis	So, we have three production lines, running on three shifts in twenty-four hours. ② From pouring raw material into it, to bottling and packaging, all consistent manufacturing by machines. ③	我們一共有三條生產線,每天24小時運作,分成3班。從原料倒入,到裝瓶、裝箱,全部機器一貫化作業。
Sophia	The machine is a new one?	機器是新的?
Louis	Yes, we just replaced the old one last year. ④Imported from Japan. ⑤	對呀,去年剛換的。是日本原裝進口的。
Sophia	It must costs a lot.	成本很高吧。
Louis	Because we want to provide customers the best. Have a look at the pictures on the wall.	因為我們想要給消費者最好的。看看牆上的圖。
Sophia	Looks like process pictures.	好像是工藝流程圖。
Louis	Correct! The pictures clearly show our process of manufacturing. ⑥	答對了!圖表清楚表達了我們的製造過程。
Sophia	Very interesting, thank you, Louis. I am impressed as ten years ago.	真有意思。謝謝你,路易士。我還是和十年前一樣印象深刻。
Louis	You are welcome, let's go upstairs for a cup of coffee.	不客氣。那麼我們上樓喝杯咖啡吧。

實用應答小撇步 **1**

① Let me show you the newly-built museum / Let him take you to see the production(process) / Let me take her to visit the construction site

讓我帶大家參觀新落成的博物館吧／讓他帶您去看生產流程吧／讓我帶她去參觀工地吧

② We are running on two shifts at the factory / There are only security guards when getting to the time to leave / There are people stay to take care the company all day long

我們工廠實行兩班制／公司到了下班時間就只剩警衛／公司整天都有人留守

③ They are all handmade / First they are picked by people, bottling by machines, then packaging be people again

全部是手工製成／首先由人工挑選，然後由機器裝瓶，再由人工裝箱

④ Bought a new one last month / It is going to be eliminated / We are going to purchase in the future

上個月剛買新的／這是將要被淘汰的／未來將要採購的

⑤ This is going to exporting to USA / Transported in Hong Kong / The goods are assembled and installed at Taiwan, then exported to worldwide

這是將要輸出到美國的／在香港轉運的／貨物來台灣被組裝後，又輸出到世界各地

⑥ Our company's wastewater treatment process is fully introduced in this presentation / The most new products are completely collected in the product catalog / Company history is all covered on this post

簡報完整介紹了公司的汙水回收過程／產品目錄完整收錄了我們的最新產品／這張海報涵蓋了公司歷史

對話 2 Conversation 2

Matthew	Hi, Quincy. What brought you here?	嗨，昆西。是什麼風把你吹來了？
Quincy	For staying close with production schedule. ①	為了盯生產進度囉。
Matthew	You are doing a good job.	辛苦你了。
Quincy	The production speed seems a little bit slower today?	今天機器好像生產速度比較慢？
Matthew	Yes, we arrange the routine maintenance tomorrow. ② If there is still a problem, we probably will report to worthless. ③	是的，安排了明天維修。如果還是有問題，恐怕要報廢了。
Quincy	Renew the production machine? Then the production process will behind schedule again?	換一台新的生產機器？那麼生產進度又要落後了？
Matthew	I am afraid so. I don't want this to happen either. ④	恐怕是的。我也不希望這事情發生。
Quincy	This is really terrible, you know, its peak season is in the second half. ⑤	真糟糕，你也知道，下半年是旺季。
Matthew	Yes, I know that.	我知道。
Quincy	Is there any way you can do?	有什麼辦法沒有？

Matthew	How about this? After the other production line finished, we can use it to produce this product.	要不這樣，等下另外一條生產線結束，就用它來生產這項產品吧。
Quincy	What a great idea!	太好的點子了！
Matthew	Just keeping trying everything in a desperate situation. I will give it a try, so don't get your hopes up too high. ⑥	這叫死馬當活馬醫。我也只是試試看，別抱太大希望。
Quincy	OK. Right, I go to the Design Department for a minute.	知道了。對了，我去一下設計部門。
Matthew	What's wrong?	怎麼了？
Quincy	Just checking on the progress, we are going to attend the annual exhibition next month and I don't want to rush it again. ⑦	只是確認一下工作進度而已，下個月就要參加一年一度的展覽了，我可不希望到時候又再趕工。

實用應答小撇步 2

① For speeding up delivery process / For new product launch / For increasing sales / For decreasing inventory

為了加快出貨進度／為了新產品發佈會／為了提高業績／為了減少庫存

② Inventory count is arranged tomorrow / The factory will proceed fire inspection next week / Total factory disinfection is scheduled at next month

安排了明天清點庫存／預計下周進行工廠消防安檢／安排了下個月進行工廠全面消毒

③ I am afraid these parts would be recycled / I am afraid the product would been removed from shelves / I am afraid this dispute could only be solved through going to court

零件恐怕要被回收了／產品恐怕要下架了／糾紛恐怕要上法院才能解決了

④ Company executives don't want to see we make this kind of mistake again / The department supervisor doesn't want you to continue

公司高層不希望看見我們再犯這樣的錯誤／部門主管不希望你再繼續負責這件專案了

⑤ This season is off-season / The shipment this month is the most among a year / The defect rate is the lowest in this week among whole month

這一季是淡季／這個月是一年裡出貨量最多的月份／這周的不良率是本月最低的

⑥ He only can do his best to try / The only thing you can do is giving up after tried hard / Don't give up easily

他也只能盡力試試看／努力後還是不行的話，你也只好放棄／不要輕言放棄

⑦ We are going to attend biennial beauty exhibition next week / It is the semi-annual International Computer Exhibition three months later / It is Ambiente after the Chinese New Year

下周就要參加兩年一度的美容用品大展／三個月後就是半年一次的國際電腦展／農曆過年後就是法蘭克福家庭用品展

💬 單字與句型

1. construction site　工地
2. eliminate _v._　淘汰
   也有刪除、排除、消除的意思。

   Can we ever eliminate poverty from the world?

   我們能完全消除貧窮嗎？

   I was eliminated from the 200 meters in the semi-finals.

   我在200公尺的半決賽中被淘汰了。

3. stay close with　緊盯著
4. the second half　下半年
5. rush　趕工
   動詞、名詞與形容詞同型。動詞有追趕、撲、奔、闖、搶購的意思，名詞有
   魯莽的意思。這個字用在植物界，就是燈心草的名字。形容詞則有匆忙的、
   急需的意思。

   The manager gave us a rush job.　主管給了我們一個很緊急的專案。

6. remove from shelve　下架
   同義詞有recall，召回。相反詞，上架的英文為on shelves.

   One hundred AA cars were recalled for air conditioner part problem.
   一百輛AA的車子因為冷氣零件的問題而被召回。

   Get your product onto retail shelves.　讓你的產品在零售店裡上架。

7. off-season　淡季
   也可以寫成 non-peak season（非旺季），旺季就是peak season。

8. defect rate　不良率；良率寫作yield rate或defect-free rate。

9. biennial　兩年一次
   quarterly 是三個月一次（一季一次）。twice a year(semi-annual)半年一
   次。triennial是三年一次。quadrennial為四年一度。quinquennial是五年
   一次。every ten years則是每十年一次，其中的ten可以換做其他數字，用
   以表達每N年一次。

💬 練習題

A: I heard that our company's cell phone is _____.

B: Yes, it happens _____. Now is _____.

A: Oh My God! The _____ is really high.

B: The sales of _____ could be declined again.

A: This company is going to be _____.

B: I think we need to look for a new job.

A：聽說我們公司的手機產品被<u>下架</u>了。

B：對呀，<u>每三個月</u>就發生一次。現在是<u>旺季</u>耶。

A：天啊！<u>不良率</u>太高了。

B：<u>下半年</u>業績又會衰退了。

A：公司就要被<u>淘汰</u>了吧。

B：我看我們還是去找新工作吧。

💬 解 答

1. removed from shelves

2. quarterly，peak season

3. defect rate

4. the second half

5. eliminated

Unit 02 介紹工廠環境 Introducing Environment

對話 1 Conversation 1

Viv	Morning, Yvonne. How's your flight yesterday?	早安，伊馮娜。昨天的飛機還順利嗎？
Yvonne	It delayed by two hours at Moscow, except that, everything was good. ①	班機在莫斯科延遲了兩個小時。除此之外，一切都好。
Viv	I hope you don't have headache right now.	希望妳現在不會感到頭疼。
Yvonne	Maybe I take an aspirin later. So, where you are going to show me around today? ②	也許我等會兒會吃顆阿斯匹靈。今天要帶我從哪裡參觀起呢？
Viv	This is your first time visiting Taiwan Branch, isn't it? ③	這是妳第一次參觀台灣的分公司，對吧？
Yvonne	Yes. Since it finished, I haven't got any chance to be here before.	是的。從蓋好後，我一直沒有機會過來參觀。
Viv	So, let's start with the surrounding environment. ④ The factory is surrounded by one thousand square meters greening. ⑤	那我們從周圍環境開始介紹吧。工廠被1千平方米的綠化環境圍繞著。

Yvonne	This is amazing!	真是不可思議！
Viv	Indeed. We not only set up many solar panels in order to saving energy, but also recycle and reuse the wasted water in park. ⑥	是的。我們也架設了很多太陽能板，儲存電力之外，園區裡的汙水都回收再利用。
Yvonne	Reuse? Such as?	重新利用？例如呢？
Viv	For example, the water for toilet flushing, the pond, and plant watering system.	例如沖馬桶的水、魚池、植物灑水系統等等。
Yvonne	It's well advanced! By the way, why the roofs are pitched?	好先進！對了，為什麼屋頂都是斜的？
Viv	So we can collect rainwater in raining days and it also be recycled and reused. ⑦	因為這樣可以在雨天收集雨水，同樣可以回收再利用。
Yvonne	I am really impressed.	我真是大開眼界。
Viv	The wood is used environment-friendly coatings, so there is no hazardous material which is harmful to human health. ⑧	還有木材都使用了生態塗料，不會產生有害物質危害人體健康。
Yvonne	I will definitely report to the European Headquarter. ⑨	我一定會回報歐洲總公司。
Viv	I can provide you some information.	我可以把相關資料提供給妳。
Yvonne	That would be wonderful.	那就太好了。

實用應答小撇步 1

① The plane landed three hours earlier than scheduled / The train was delayed for five hours / The High Speed Rail was suspended for one hour due to mechanical failure

班機提前三小時降落／火車延誤了五個小時／高鐵因機械故障，停駛一個小時

② Let's start factory tour from visiting production line (design center) / Let me show you around from Product Display Center / Sorry, the R&D center is no unauthorized access prohibited.

我們從生產線（設計中心）開始參觀起／讓我帶各位從產品展示中心開始參觀起／抱歉，研發中心禁止參觀

③ This is her first time visiting Taiwan / This is my first time coming to Frankfurt / How many times have you been to Shanghai?

這是她第一次來到台灣／這是我第一次到法蘭克福／這是你第幾次來上海？

④ I will introduce this factory from the history / Please start with the factory's environmental conservation / May I ask you start with how the factory does recycling?

我從工廠歷史開始介紹起吧／請從工廠環境保育開始說起吧／請你從工廠如何做資源回收開始說起吧

⑤ The factory locates at Southern Taiwan Science Park / There are many beautiful landscapes in the factory / Our factory is around by shoe factories / We are the only one food manufacturing company here

工廠位於南科園區內／工廠內有許多美麗的造景／我們工廠被製鞋的工廠圍繞著／這裡只有我們一家食品製造公司

⑥ We use energy-efficient LED lighting in our factory / Their factory use a lot of automatic equipment

我們工廠使用LED省電照明／他們工廠使用許多自動化設備

⑦ can be used to generate electrical power from the wind / can reduce waste generation

可以從風力產生電力／可以減少垃圾產生

⑧ It doesn't cause air pollution / It doesn't cause property loss

不會造成空氣汙染／不會造成財產損失

⑨ She will definitely report to her manager / I will definitely put in a good word for you / Will you definitely forgive me?

她一定會上報主管／我一定會替你說好話／你一定會原諒我嗎？

單字與句型

1. solar panel　太陽能板
2. recycle *v.*　資源回收
3. reuse *v.*　再利用
   環保裡經常提到的3R就是Reduce，減量。Recycle，回收。Reuse，再利用。
4. toilet flushing 馬桶的沖水
   沖水馬桶寫作a flush toilet。low-flush toilet就是台灣所謂的省水馬桶。Please flush after using，就是上完廁所要記得沖水的意思。馬桶不通則是寫作toilet is clogged。
5. environment-friendly coating　環保塗料
   環保還可以簡寫成eco-friendly。
6. hazardous *adj.*　危險的、有害的
7. no unauthorized access prohibited　未經授權，禁止入內
   這句話還可以這樣說：No unauthorized entry、No access without permission。
8. landscape *n.*　景觀
   其他延伸用法有，landscape painting，風景畫。landscape design，景觀設計。
9. energy-efficient　省能源、省電
10. waste generation　廢棄物產生
    關於廢棄物（俗稱的垃圾）描述，常用的還有industrial waste，事業／工業廢棄物，指得是事業體（公司或工廠）產生的垃圾；以及general waste，一般廢棄物。
11. air pollution　空氣汙染
    水汙染寫作water pollution。
12. put in a good word for somebody　替某人說好話

練習題

A: Look. The _____ is so beautiful.

B: Yes. It looks no _____ here.

A: And eco-friendly. I see _____ and LED lighting.

B: It must be _____.

A: But it says "_____" here.

B: Then we should leave.

A: By the way, is the _____ again?

B: Yes. I will find someone to fix it later.

A：你看。這景觀好美啊。

B：對呀。看來沒有什麼空氣汙染。

A：還很環保。我看到了太陽能板和LED燈。

B：一定很省能源。

A：不過這裡寫著「未經授權，不得進入」。

B：那就走吧。

A：對了，家裡馬桶又堵住了？

B：是呀。我晚點找人來修吧。

解　答

1. landscape

2. air pollution

3. solar panels

4. energy-efficient

5. No unauthorized entry / No access without permission / No unauthorized access prohibited

6. toilet clogged

Unit 03 介紹附近環境 Introducing the Neighborhood

對話 1 Conversation 1

Fergus	Welcome on board, Thomas!	歡迎加入我們公司，湯瑪斯！
Thomas	Thanks, Fergus.	謝謝你，佛格斯。
Fergus	If you need any help, just name it. ①	有什麼問題儘管開口。
Thomas	I would like to know where everybody goes out to lunch. ②	我想知道大家都到哪裡吃午餐？
Fergus	There are many food stalls and cafeterias nearby, so, a great deal of options for you. ③ Some stores even open at morning, so you can also have breakfast there.	這附近很多小吃攤，自助餐廳也有，任君選擇。有些店早上也開，可以在那裡吃早餐。
Thomas	If I work overtime, what time does the last bus leave? ④	假如加班的話，最晚一班公車是幾點鐘呢？
Fergus	Usually at eight o'clock. But I will suggest you go out at seven forty.	通常是八點整。但是我會建議你七點四十分出來。
Thomas	OK.	好的。
Fergus	Anything else?	還有嗎？

Thomas	I live at staff dormitory, [5] but it doesn't seem have a gym. Where you will suggest me to go to? [6]	我就住在員工宿舍，但是好像沒有健身房。你建議去哪裡運動好呢？
Fergus	There is a municipal swimming pool which takes you ten minutes to walk there. [7] There is an elementary school behind where you live, and you can jog on playground inside.	走路十分鐘有市立游泳池。你住的地方的後面有一間國小，裡面有操場可以跑步。
Thomas	Thanks, I will look around.	謝了。我會去找找。
Fergus	By the way, do you cook?	對了，你會煮飯嗎？
Thomas	If I have time on weekends.	假日的話，有時間就煮。
Fergus	Then you need to know how to get the supermarket. [8] Let me show you after work. [9]	那你需要知道超市怎麼走。下了班我帶你走一趟吧。
Thomas	That would be great.	那就太好了。

實用應答小撇步 1

① just speak out / just tell me / just let me know

儘管開口／儘管告訴我／儘管讓我知道

② Where does the Sales Department often go on a business trip? / Where does the Marketing Department usually have press conference? / Which conference room do you usually use for meeting?

業務部門通常去哪裡出差？／行銷部門通常在哪裡辦記者會？／你們通常使用哪一間會議室開會？

③ There are many similar factories nearby / It's not a very lively neighborhood / It's very convenient for everything here

這附近很多同類型的工廠／這裡不會很熱鬧／這裡什麼都很方便

④ What time does the last picking up for express? / When does the fastest shipment arrive at California? / When does the latest flight arrive at Tokyo?

最晚一次快遞收件是幾點？／貨運最快何時抵達加州？／班機最慢何時抵達東京？

⑤ He stays at the hotels which the company signed a contract with / Why don't you live at the apartment where the company rent for you? / The company provides staff dormitory to the employees who is sent to China

他出差時就住在公司簽約的酒店裡／你為什麼不住在公司為你租的公寓？／公司提供員工宿舍給派往大陸工作的員工

⑥ He asked us to go around the night market together after work / Do you know what's good to eat around here? / I suggest you go to suburbs for weekends

他約我們下班後一起去夜市逛逛／你知道這附近有什麼好吃的？／我建議你

們假日可以到郊外走走

⑦ It takes you five minutes by taxi to arrive downtown / There is an convenient store right around the corner / Take train or high-speed train first, then transfer to city bus, and you will arrive Taoyuan International Airport after forty minutes.

搭計程車5分鐘可以到達市中心／轉角有便利商店／搭火車或高鐵，再轉市內公車，40分鐘後可以抵達桃園國際機場

⑧ Let me tell you bank account opening procedures / Let him show you how to use the product / Let us take you to the airport(railway station)

讓我告訴妳銀行開戶手續／讓他示範產品如何使用／讓我們帶您們前往機場（車站）

⑨ Let me take you to there during the lunch time / He will take you to there later on / He can give you a lift (ride) on his way home

中午休息時我帶你去吧／等一下他就會帶你去／他可以回家時順路帶你一程

單字與句型

1. just name it　儘管說
   這裡的**name it**，並不是取名字的意思，而是「儘管說」的意思。

2. staff dormitory　員工宿舍
   也可以寫成**Employee dormitory**。**dormitory**也可以簡稱**dorm**。

3. gym *n.*　健身房
   有一個相似的詞，**gymnasium**，則是體育館的意思。

4. playground *n.*　操場

5. press conference　記者會
   press有媒體、記者的意思。

6. conference room　會議室
   電話會議可以簡稱**con-call**，**con**就是**conference**，會議的縮寫。

7. lively *adj.*　熱鬧　*adv.*　活潑
   形容詞與副詞同形，形容詞還有鮮明的、栩栩如生的意思；副詞有生氣勃勃地意思。

   What lively color!　多麼鮮明的顏色！

8. right around the corner　在轉角處
   這句用法還有另外兩個意思。

   I am right around the corner.

   我就快到了（並非真的就在轉角的地方，只是形容很靠近約定的地點）。

   Winter is right around the corner.　冬天就快要到來。

9. high-speed train　高速鐵路
   還可以寫成**high-speed**（**rail**或**railway**）。

10. bank account opening　銀行帳戶開戶
    open a bank account，就是開一個銀行帳戶。

11. procedure *n.*　手續、程序

12. lunch time　午餐時間、午休時間
    其他與休息相關的詞還有：**brank room**，休息室；**tea break**，享用茶點的休息時間。

🗨 練習題

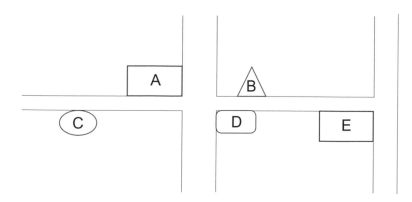

A: _____ / 體育館

B: _____ / 員工宿舍

C: _____ / 高鐵車站

D: _____ / 記者會

E: _____ / 操場

🗨 解　答

1. gymnasium

2. employee dormitory / staff dormitory

3. High-speed rail(way) / train station

4. press conference

5. playground

主題 ④ 工廠導覽 A Factory Tour

職場補給站：工廠導覽—另類的一日遊

　　不論是參觀上游供應商，或者下游的裝配廠工廠，可以說是另類的「一日遊」。在這短則數分鐘，長則一兩日行程裡，接待方要如何安排動線、內容，或者參觀的一方打定主意希望要「看到什麼」，靠的是事前的完善規劃。

　　由於本書為英語學習，以下就針對接待「說外語」的訪客，需要有哪些參觀工廠注意事項，提供意見：

❶ 先熟悉訪客的國籍背景。由於各地風俗民情不同，作息也大不相同。例如同樣的下午三、四點鐘，如果訪客是義大利人的話，可以大膽假設，他們已經在中午的時候喝過espresso了，建議可以直接開始介紹工廠，不用費事招呼下午茶事宜；但是稍作休息時，倒是可以和他們聊聊足球的議題。假如是香港或英國來的客人，最好提供一些下午茶，博得好感。但是換成日本客人的話，對方可能反而覺得花時間「享受」下午茶，不是此行的目的，反而會讓工廠被留下「不認真」的印象。

❷ 送禮的忌諱(cannot do)。對於美國人來說，用黑色的包裝紙包裝禮物，是極不吉利的。對德國客人，也避免送有尖銳稜角(sharp)的東西，同樣也是不吉利的。英國客人忌諱單價高的，因為這感覺像在賄賂他們。至於可以送的禮物，對法國人則是最好帶點藝術氣息的禮物，對美國人就送些有民俗特色的，給德國客人的，就用點心在包裝上吧。

❸ 參訪後是不是要安排餐敘(eating together)？大致上來說，如果結束時間剛好是午飯或者晚飯時間，不論是第一次見面或者已經合作多次的訪客，都會禮貌性的邀請一起餐敘；如果對方堅持不用，就不勉強。但是對日本

130

客人的話，請以第四次的答案為主，因為在日本的習慣裡，前三次的拒絕都是基於禮儀。此外，招待英、法訪客，以精緻、七八分飽為主；招待德國客人，則要切記食物最好不要剩下，否則就會給人「浪費資源(a waste of resources)」的印象。

其他和接待本國訪客時，需要留意的共同事項有：

❶ 分成小組。如果訪客人數很多，最好分成小團體(small groups)進行，讓每個人都有被照顧到的感覺。通常來說，一到三位導覽或解說員可以照顧九到十五位客人。

❷ 懂得藏拙(Hide one's inadequacy by keeping quiet)。由於被參觀中的工廠，通常都是正在作業中的狀態，所以對工廠來說，也很擔心生產線上一不小心的突發狀況，暴露在訪客面前。有經驗的工廠在動線安排上，就會懂得適當的安排與調整，甚至針對來訪的不同屬性（合作很久的客戶的參訪、合作前的參訪）都安排有不同的「曝光」程度。

Part

Five

接待國外客戶
Reception of Foreign Guests

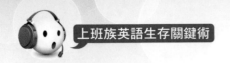

Unit 01 行程安排 Schedule Arrangement

對話 1 Conversation 1

Georgina Hey, Nicole. Can we now confirm the schedule of reception of foreign guest next week?

嗨，妮可。我們現在可以確認一下下週接待國外客人的行程嗎？

Nicole Sure.

當然可以。

Georgina First, who will go to pick him up at the airport? ①

首先，誰會去機場接機？

Nicole Michael will do that. He'll get the client to Regent Taipei, and come to visit the company one hour later. ②

麥可會去。先送客戶到晶華酒店，一個半小時後再來公司參觀。

Georgina Good. It's time for dinner after the visiting. Did you call to make a reservation at Din Tai Fung Restaurant the day before yesterday? ③

很好。參觀完也該吃晚餐了，前天妳打電話到鼎泰豐餐廳訂位了嗎？

Nicole They are fully booked, so I rescheduled to an Italian restaurant. ④

他們客滿了。我改訂一間義大利餐廳。

Georgina It seems that the client prefers French cuisine, so book a French restaurant.

客戶好像偏好法國菜，改成訂法國餐廳吧。

Nicole	Then I need to spend time on Googling where is a good place. Should we get him directly back to hotel after dinner?⑤	那我得花時間上網查一下哪一家好吃。用餐完以後直接送他回飯店嗎？
Georgina	He wanted to go to Eastern area of Taipei. Why don't you go with him after dinner?	他說想要去逛東區。不如用餐完妳陪他去吧？
Nicole	I am going to my yoga class. Let Michael go with him.	我要上瑜珈課。還是讓麥可陪他吧。
Georgina	OK.	也行。
Nicole	What time should we pick him up at the hotel the day after tomorrow? ⑥	隔天要幾點去飯店接他呢？
Georgina	The meeting starts at ten, so night-thirty.	會議是十點鐘開始，九點半吧。
Nicole	No problem. Michael takes a day off that day, so I will go to pick him up.	沒問題。麥克請假，我去接他好了。
Georgina	Thank you. After the meeting, we eat at National Palace Museum. Then we go to the airport after visiting the Museum as he wishes. ⑦	麻煩妳啦。開完會，我們一起到故宮用午餐，然後依照他希望的，參觀一下故宮，就要到機場去了。
Nicole	I hope he will satisfy with this arrangement.	希望他會滿意這個行程。

實用應答小撇步 1

① Who will be charged the schedule arrangement? / Who is responsible for picking up? / Who will be charged the restaurant reservation? 誰負責行程安排？／誰負責接送？／誰負責預約餐廳？

② Have lunch with the client after the meeting / Get the client to anywhere he/she wants to go after dinner / The client will go to the airport directly after visiting tourist attractions

會議後再與客戶吃午餐／晚餐後送客戶到想去的地方／客戶參觀景點後將直接去機場

③ Did you book the ticket and hotel? / Did you arrange the schedule for tomorrow? / Is he ready for tomorrow's presentation? / Please confirm with Susan if she booked the ticket of business trip for next month

你訂好機票與酒店了嗎？／妳安排好明天的行程了嗎？／他準備好明天的簡報了嗎？／請與蘇珊確認下個月的出差的機票訂好了嗎？

④ There's an one hour wait / There's only one room left / The ticket is sold out 要等一個小時才有位子／酒店只剩一間空房了／機票賣光了

⑤ Come directly to the office after picking up at the airport? / Go directly to the airport after city tour? / Come back to the office again for meeting after lunch?

接機後直接到公司嗎？／市區觀光後直接到機場嗎？／午餐後又回到公司開會嗎？

⑥ When is the pick-up (see-off) time? / When does the meeting start?

幾點去接（送）機？／會議幾點開始？

⑦ Go to the airport after city sightseeing / After picking up, we go to visit the factory first / We go to the shopping mall before seeing off

參觀一下市區就要去機場了／接機後我們要先參觀工廠／送機前我們去一下購物中心

對話 2 | Conversation **2**

Randolf	What do you need, Ivy?	有什麼事嗎？艾薇。
Ivy	It's about the schedule of our German clients, there are some things I need to confirm with you.	關於明天那批德國客人的行程，有些問題我想再與您確認。
Randolf	Isn't it too late?	現在確認不會太晚嗎？
Ivy	I am really sorry. We were preparing the press conference since few days ago.①	很抱歉。前幾天我們都在準備昨天的記者會。
Randolf	This is terrible.	真是糟糕。
Ivy	Only some changes of the transportation part, other parts should be fine. ②	只有交通工具的部分有異動，其他應該沒問題。
Randolf	Go ahead.	說吧。
Ivy	Can we not take High Speed Rail after picking up, but domestic flight to Tainan?③	接機後我們不坐高鐵，改搭國內班機去台南可以嗎？
Randolf	We are going to visit Southern Taiwan Science Park, so we'd better take High Speed Rail and get off at Tainan Station.④⑤	第一天要參觀南科，所以還是搭高鐵在台南站下車吧。
Ivy	But colleagues don't have time to pick us up.	但是同事沒有時間來接我們。

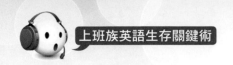
Randolf	We can take a taxi and go there by ourselves.⑥	我們可以自己搭計程車過去。
Ivy	Then that would be fine.	那就沒問題了。
Randolf	After the visiting, make sure there are Managers from Southern Science Park branch will go to dinner with us.	參觀之後，要確保南科分公司有主管陪同共進晚餐。
Ivy	OK. By the way, I just received the e-mail from the client, he wants us to help arrange a personal schedule. He wishes to go to a stage play or an opera.⑦	好的。對了，我剛才收到客戶來信，第二天晚上想要我們幫忙安排私人行程。他希望看場舞台劇或聽歌劇。
Randolf	This seems difficult. Please check if you can find any related play like that, or ask the colleagues at Southern Science Park branch to help.	這可難了。查查台南或者高雄有沒有相關的演出，或者請南部的同事幫忙吧。
Ivy	OK. That's it, thank you.	好的。那就這樣吧。謝謝您。

實用應答小撇步 2

① They are preparing materials for presentation these two days / We have been preparing for the shipment since last week / We have been working overtime since this month

這兩天他們都在準備簡報資料／從上週起我們都在準備出貨／這一個月來我們都加班

② Only the return ticket changed the date / Only less one person / Only one more day on business trip

只有回程機票改期／只有人數少一人／只有出差天數多一天

③ Take cheap flights to Paris / Take Shinkansen to Tokyo / Take cruise

改搭廉價航空去巴黎／改搭新幹線去東京／改搭郵輪

④ Visit Taipei one-o-one tomorrow / Visit down(up)stream firms the day after tomorrow / Visit Singapore Headhunter next week

明天要參觀台北101／後天要參觀下（上）游廠商的工廠／下週要參觀新加坡獵人頭公司

⑤ Take Taiwan Railway and get off at Hsinchu Station / Take European cheap airlines and arrive London after transferring at Madrid / Take the Beijing–Guangzhou High-Speed Line and get off at Guangzhou Station

搭台鐵到新竹站下車／搭歐洲廉價航空在馬德里轉機後抵達倫敦／搭京廣高鐵到廣州站下車

⑥ They can take international flights / You can take a shuttle bus and get there／他們可以搭國際班機去／你們可以搭接駁巴士過去／我們可以晚一點自己走過去

⑦ I wish to buy some local special products / She wishes to see Cloud Gate Dance Theatre / Do you prefer a city tour or go to a shopping mall?

我希望買一些特產／她希望看雲門舞集／你希望去市區觀光還是購物中心？

🗩 單字與句型

1. reschedule 重新安排
    reschedule為動詞,重新安排的意思。

    We have rescheduled your shipment to next Monday.　我們重新安排了出貨的時間到下周一。

2. seem *v.* 似乎是
    seem有以下四種用法:

    1) 人 + seem + 形容詞　He seems happy.　他看起來好像是快樂的。

    2) It seems that + 子句　It seems that tomorrow will be a raining day. 似乎明天會是一個雨天。

    3) seem + like + 名詞　The flower seems like a human face.　那朵花看起來好像一個人的臉。

    4) seem + to + 動詞　You seem to be the only woman in this company.　妳好像是這間公司裡唯一的女性。

3. reservation *n.* 預約、訂位
    也有保留的意思,此為名詞,動詞是reserve。餐廳訂位可以說making a reservation或booking a table。

4. tourist attraction 旅遊觀光景點
    attract是吸引的動詞型,attraction是其名詞,解釋成吸引力,延伸為對觀光客來說,有吸引力的旅遊景點。

5. sold out 賣光了

6. pick-up / see-off 接/送
    I am going to see my cousin off at bus station tomorrow night at eight.　我明天晚上八點要去巴士站送我表親。

7. shuttle bus 接駁巴士
    shuttle有穿梭的意思,所以穿梭於定點之間的巴士就叫做shuttle bus。

8. local special product 特產品、土產

練習題

Schedules of business trip on 20th, December:

12月20日出差行程：

8 AM	Breakfast
8:30 AM	Take the _____ to Business Center
2:00 PM	_____.
4:00 PM	_____ tomorrow's meeting.
6:00 PM	Dinner
10:00 PM	Back to hotel

上午8點	早餐
上午8點30分	搭接駁巴士到商務中心
下午2點	餐廳訂位
下午4點	重新安排明天的會議
下午6點	晚餐
下午10點	返回飯店

解 答

1. shuttle bus
2. making a reservation / booking a table
3. reschedule

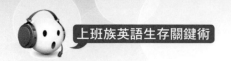
Unit 02 地區觀光 Regional Tourism

對話 1 Conversation 1

Vince	Hi, Wesley. I have heard that you are from Kaohsiung, would you mind doing me a favor? ①	嗨，衛斯理。聽說你是高雄人，可以幫我一個忙嗎？
Wesley	Sure, what is it?	可以啊，是什麼？
Vince	The American clients will visit us next week, so we are planning to arrange sightseeing tours at Southern. ②	下週美國客戶要來拜訪我們，我們打算安排南部的觀光行程。
Wesley	Oh, I see. It's easy, what kind of tours they want? ③	哦，這樣啊。很容易，他們想要什麼樣的行程？
Vince	What do you mean by that?	什麼意思？
Wesley	There are many kinds of tours, historic sites, local features, shopping centers and art exhibitions, etc. etc.	觀光有分很多種啊，歷史古蹟、當地特色、購物中心、藝術展覽…等等的行程。
Vince	Got you. Probably divided into two groups, one to local landscapes and the other to art exhibition and shopping malls. ④	懂了。可能分兩團，一團去當地風景，另一團去藝術展覽和購物吧。
Wesley	Good plan! Then you must not miss Love River at night, Liuohe	好計畫！那麼你一定不能錯過晚上的愛河、六合夜

	Tourist Night Market, Ferry and Cijin Harbor. [5] You must don't miss the local sea food and soy tomato.	市、渡輪與旗津港。旗津有許多當地海鮮和醬油番茄，不可錯過。
Vince	Soy tomato?	醬油番茄？
Wesley	It's a plate of fresh cut tomato, and it comes with a plate of sauce made from ginger, soy sauce and sugar.	就是新鮮番茄切片，和一盤薑末和醬油、糖混合的調味料。
Vince	Sounds delicious. How about the art exhibition and shopping malls?	聽起來很可口。藝術展覽和購物中心呢？
Wesley	There are many famous Department Stores at Sanduo Shopping District, but Dream Mall is the biggest one. There is a free shuttle bus from Metro Station which can get you there.	三多商圈有很多知名百貨公司，不過夢時代是最大的購物中心。從捷運站可以搭免費接駁車過去。
Vince	Sounds very convenient and money-saving.	聽起來很方便且省錢。
Wesley	As art experiences, you can go to Kaohsiung Museum of Fine Arts, The Pier-2 Art Center or even Kaohsiung Museum of Military Dependents Village to experience the endemic culture of Taiwan. [6]	至於藝術體驗，你們可以去高雄市立美術館、駁二藝術特區，還有到眷村文化館體驗台灣特有的文化。
Vince	What a wonderful trip! Thank you, Wesley, I think I will lead the art group by myself.	真是精采！謝謝你，衛斯理，我想我會親自帶領藝術團。
Wesley	Then wish you have a good time. [7]	那就祝你玩得盡興囉。

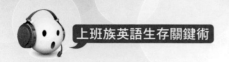

實用應答小撇步 **1**

① I come from Texas, U.S.A(America) / May I ask where are you from? / My hometown is Scotland

我來自美國德州／請問你是哪裡人？／我的家鄉是蘇格蘭

② They plan to arrange a hot spring tour in suburban Taipei / We plan to manage a tour of historic sites in Tainan / Will you arrange a tour of Taiwan's offshore islands?

他們打算安排一個台北市近郊的溫泉行程／我們想要安排台南古蹟導覽行程／你們會安排台灣離島行程嗎？

③ What kind of hotel do you expect? / What kind of city tours do they expect? / Which flight they are going to take to arrive Taiwan?

你們希望什麼樣的飯店？／他們期待什麼樣的市區觀光行程？／他們準備搭哪一班航班抵達台灣？

④ We needs to divide into three shifts(stages) / It might need two cars

我們需要分成三梯次／可能要兩部車

⑤ You must experience it / You have to taste this / It's a shame if you miss it

你一定要體驗／你一定要嚐嚐／錯過可惜

⑥ To National Palace Museum experience Chinese culture / To night market eat local cuisine of Taiwan / To Kenting experience the beach of Southern Taiwan

到故宮體驗中國文化／到夜市吃台灣道地小吃／到墾丁體驗南台灣的海灘

⑦ Wish you a nice trip / Have a very pleasant journey

祝你有個愉快的旅途／祝你順風

對話 2 | Conversation 2

Nat	Hi, Cherry, welcome to Taiwan.	嗨，雀莉，歡迎你來到台灣。
Cherry	Thanks.	謝謝。
Nat	I hope you don't get bored of the meeting these days.	這幾天的會議希望妳不會覺得無聊。
Cherry	Once you get used to it. You know, I also travel a lot when I am in the U.S.A.	習慣就好了。你知道的，我在美國也經常出差。
Nat	Your department seems busy.	你們部門似乎很忙。
Cherry	Right, may I ask you, what does Ximending look like?	對了，我想問你，西門町是個什麼樣的地方？
Nat	Well, in my opinion, it's a place full of youthfulness and energy. ① Young people go there and look for suitable clothes and accessories that kind of stuff. You could take a trip if you like it.②	嗯，在我看來是充滿年輕活力的地方。年輕人在那裡找尋適合的衣服、首飾等東西。如果你喜歡可以走一趟。
Cherry	Like a flea market?	類似跳蚤市場？
Nat	Part of it, but they also have stores. You could find something cheap and suitable for your style.	一部份，也有店面。可以碰運氣找到便宜又適合自己風格的東西。

Cherry	What if for sightseeing? I think I need a place for fresh air.④	如果是看風景呢？我想我需要找一個呼吸新鮮空氣的地方。
Nat	You can go to Beitou, Yangming-shan, and Maokong in Taipei City. As at New Taipei City, you can go to Danshuei, Bitan, Jiufen, and Wulai.	台北市有北投、陽明山、貓空。新北市有淡水、碧潭、九份、烏來都不錯。
Cherry	Can I get there by metro?⑤	捷運可以到嗎？
Nat	You can take buses, too. I'll let my secretary print a traffic guide, if you need it.⑥	也有巴士，如果妳需要，我讓祕書印一份交通資訊給妳。
Cherry	That would be wonderful. What special local products I could buy?⑦	那就太好了。我可以買到什麼特產呢？
Nat	They have tea in Maokong, and some souvenirs in Jiufen and Wulai.	貓空有茶葉，九份和烏來也有些紀念品。
Cherry	Wow, that sounds exactly I am looking for. Thank you, Nat.	哇，聽起來正是我要的。謝謝你啦，納特。

實用應答小撇步 **2**

① A town with natural scenery / An artistic building (community) / A tropical island

充滿自然風光的城鎮／充滿藝術氣息的建築物（社區）／充滿熱帶風情的島嶼

② I can show (take) you if you like / He can arrange if you guys want to go / Can you tell us how to get there?

如果你喜歡我可以帶你去／你們想去的話他可以安排／可以告訴我們怎麼到達嗎？

③ I need a business hotel / Do you need a map of this city? / He needs a tour guide for half day (a one-day city tour)

我需要找一間商務酒店／你需要這個城市的地圖嗎？／他需要一個半日的導遊（城市一日遊導覽）

④ What kind of transportation we can take? / What's the train's timetable? / Need to transfer?

我們可以搭什麼交通工具？／有幾點的火車可以搭？／要轉車嗎？

⑤ He can prepare a tourism events calendar for your reference / I can help you book three train tickets for tomorrow / Can you help call a taxi to get me to the airport?

他可以準備一份觀光年曆給你參考／我可以幫你預訂三張明日的火車票／你可以幫我叫計程車送我去機場嗎？

⑥ Do you want to buy some souvenirs? / I would like to give small gifts to my colleagues, what should I buy? / He wishes to buy some folk-style home decorations

你想買些紀念品嗎？／我想送同事小禮物，應該買些什麼呢？／他希望買些民俗風的家居裝飾品

💬 單字與句型

1. divided into　分成

   divide可以想成是除法的概念。

   Please divide the apples among the children. 請把蘋果均分給孩童們。

   If you divide five into thirty-five (divide thirty-five by five), you will get seven.　如果你拿5去除35（35除以5），你會得到7。

2. local landscape　當地風景、本土景色

3. endemic *adj.*　特有的

4. suburban *adj.*　郊區的、市郊的

   此單詞形容詞和名詞同形；名詞是郊區居民的意思。

   相反詞，市中心的則寫作downtown。

5. historic site　古蹟、歷史遺址

6. offshore island　離島

7. in my opinion　我的意見是⋯

   相同意思的表達方式還有：The way I see it, From where I stand, As I see it

8. youthfulness *n.*　青春

9. accessory *n.*　配件、手飾

10. flea market　跳蚤市場

    也寫作swap meet，直譯的意思是滿足交換；也就是讓人將自己多餘的東西拿出來和有需要的人交易。

11. souvenir *n.*　紀念品

12. tropical *adj.*　熱帶的

    或寫作tropic，熱帶為the tropics。

💬 練習題

- There are many _____ views and _____ in _____ .
- Please _____ the gifts among colleagues.
- These _____ are uncommon.
- Do you like to go to a _____ (a _____)?
- _____ , you don't need those _____ .

- 離島有許多特有的景色和古蹟。
- 請把禮物均分給同事們。
- 這些當地風景在台灣並不常見。
- 你喜歡逛跳蚤市場嗎？
- 我的意見是，你不需要這些首飾。

💬 解 答

1. endemic
2. historic sites
3. offshore islands
4. divided
5. local landscapes
6. swap meet / flea market
7. In my opinion / The way I see it / From where I stand / As I see it
8. accessories

Unit 03 贈送紀念品 Giving Souvenirs

對話 1 Conversation 1

Annabel	Hi, Dora, want to join us for lunch?	朵拉，要和我們一起去吃午餐嗎？
Dora	Sure, wait a minute, let me get my purse.	好啊，等等我拿一下錢包。
Annabel	Did you get the gift ready for next month's client visiting?	下個月客戶來訪的見面禮準備好了沒有？
Dora	You are well informed, knowing that I am bothered by that.[①]	妳消息真靈通，知道我為這個煩惱。
Annabel	I am all ears.	説來聽聽。
Dora	My supervisor, David, is always not satisfied with my suggestions.	我的主管，大衛，老是不滿意我的建議。
Annabel	What did you suggest?	妳建議哪些紀念品？
Dora	Pineapple pie, Alishan tea, and Kinmen Kaoliang Liquor.	鳳梨酥、阿里山茶葉、金門高粱。
Annabel	They are all regional famous products of Taiwan. Why he doesn't like them? [②]	這些都是台灣的名產。為什麼他不喜歡呢？

Dora	He said that the client prefers something with artistic sense, not food.③	他說客戶喜歡有藝術感的東西，不要送吃的。
Annabel	Well, it does make sense. Some clients are fastidious about food, so it's hard to buy the right thing to please them.④⑤	嗯，聽起來很有道理。有些客戶對吃的也很挑剔呢，很難買對東西討他們歡心。
Dora	Would you provide some suggestions? I have been racking my brains trying to find the answer.⑥	給點意見吧，我已經絞盡腦汁了。
Annabel	Let me think, an artwork. Right, how about a souvenir from National Palace Museum?	讓我想想，藝術品。對了，故宮的紀念品怎麼樣？
Dora	Great idea!	好點子！
Annabel	Just make a list of prices and types; then, let him decide.⑦	列出價錢、款式的清單，讓他去決定吧。
Dora	This is a wonderful answer. Thanks, Annabel.	這是個好方法。謝謝妳，安娜貝爾。

實用應答小撇步 1

① How did you know that? / Who told you that? / I heard it on the grapevine / No gossip at workplace

妳從哪裡知道的？／誰告訴你的？／我從小道消息聽到的／辦公室裡別談八卦

② They are famous Taiwanese celebrities / They are all Taiwan famous landmarks / All I suggested are Taiwan famous TV shows(programs)

他們都是台灣的知名藝人／這些都是台灣知名景點／我建議的都是台灣最受歡迎的電視節目

③ She likes handmade stuffs / Do you prefer the original works? / I prefer well-known brands

她喜歡手工的東西／你喜歡原創的作品嗎？／我偏好名牌

④ Some clients really care about the packaging of the gift / The client is not satisfied with the staying hotel / The client is impressed by the gift we gave

有些客戶對禮物的包裝很在意／客戶對住宿的酒店不滿意／客人對我們送的禮物印象深刻

⑤ It's hard to please your own boss / I am a thorn in her flesh / He will try his best to remove his enemies at the office

很難討自己的老闆歡心／我是她的眼中釘／他盡力要除掉辦公室裡與他為敵的人

⑥ She looks exhausted / I have done my best / You already tried whatever you can

她已經累壞了／我已經盡最大努力了／你已經試過任何辦法了

⑦ Please give me the catalog so I can choose gifts for clients / Please give me the receipt of purchasing souvenirs / Please provide me the preferences of clients, so I can choose gifts

請給我目錄，好讓我挑選給客戶的禮物／請給我購買紀念品的收據／請提供客戶的喜好，好決定禮物

對話 2 Conversation 2

Andrew	Jeanie, it was nice to meet you. Thank you for the gift you guys gave me.	珍妮，很高興認識妳。還有謝謝你們送我的禮物。
Jeanie	You are welcome. We hope that you like this gift. ①	不客氣。希望你會喜歡這個禮物
Andrew	I forget the meaning of them again, would you mind introducing it again?	我又忘了這個瓷器的意涵，妳介意再介紹一次嗎？
Jeanie	Not at all. This was bought at Yingge Ceramics Museum. ②	完全不介意。這個是在鶯歌陶瓷博物館買的。
Andrew	Yes, I remember that. Why they are wearing these clothes?	是的，我記得。為什麼他們穿著這種衣服？
Jeanie	The woman is wearing cheongsam and the man is wearing Chinese tunic suit. They were popular in Qing Dynasty and Minguo Period of China.	女生穿的叫旗袍，男生穿的叫中山裝。流行於清朝和民國時期。
Andrew	Oh, I have heard of cheongsam. This is what it looks like.	哦，我聽過旗袍。原來就是長這樣。
Jeanie	Right. Isn't it cute?	是的。可愛吧？
Andrew	It is special.	是很特別。
Jeanie	Red represents joy. We know that	紅色代表喜慶的意思。我

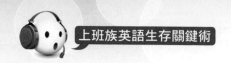
	you and your wife just got married, so that's why we picked red color one.③	們知道您和您太太剛結婚，所以特地選了紅色。
Andrew	Thank you so much. You are really thoughtful.④	非常謝謝你們。想得真是太周到了。
Jeanie	You are welcome. Oh, right, this couple is also salt and pepper shakers.	哪裡。喔，對了。這一對還是鹽與胡椒罐喔。
Andrew	I see. I think I saw the holes on their heads.	原來如此。我看見他們頭上的洞了。
Jeanie	At least you can use them to decorate your dining table.⑤	至少可以裝飾一下餐桌。
Andrew	You are right. They will come in handy when we entertain our family on Christmas.⑥	妳說對了。剛好聖誕節招待家人時可以派上用場。
Jeanie	I am glade that you like them.⑦	我很高興你喜歡它們。

實用應答小撇步 2

① Hope you will enjoy this bottle of wine / Hope this gift can be the witness of our friendship / Hope you enjoyed this meeting

希望你享受這瓶紅酒／希望這個禮物作為我們友好的見證／希望你喜歡這次的會面

② This was carefully selected by us / Here is a little something for you / We spent a little time on looking for this chic gift

這個是我們精心挑選的／這個是我們的一點心意／我們花了一點時間尋找這件別緻的禮物

③ Green means peace / In the old times the color yellow was mostly reserved for the royal family / Purple is a Royal color in the UK

綠色代表和平／黃色在古中國只被皇室使用／紫色在英國代表皇室

④ You are considerate / Thank you for your hospitality

你們真是貼心／謝謝你們的款待

⑤ It can furnish and decorate the office / Maybe it can be hung on the wall / It can be shared with everyone

可以擺設在辦公室／也許可以掛在牆上／可以大家一起享用

⑥ We just need it to adorn our office / I just need a gift like this

正好我們辦公室需要它來點綴／我正需要一件這樣的禮物

⑦ Our Chairman is truly glad that you come here to visit / They feel greatly honored to have you here

我們董事長很高興你們來訪／他們很榮幸接待你們

單字與句型

1. Pineapple pie　鳳梨酥
   pie也可以寫成cake。

2. Kaoliang *n.*　高粱
   高粱農作物的英文是sorghum，此為其漢語拼音，意旨高粱酒。

3. regional famous product　地方特產、名產

4. grapevine *n.*　小道消息
   原意是葡萄藤的意思，藉此比喻一層一層的情報網，也就是所謂的「小道消息」。

5. celebrity *n.*　藝人
   這個單詞也有名人（名流）的意思。其他相關單詞有：

   start，明星（指歌星或影星，甚至運動明星）；如果要特別區分，singer是歌星，movie / TV start則是電影／電視明星的意思。

   idol，偶像（崇拜的對象）。

6. original work　原創的作品
   仿冒品寫作copy，動名詞同形。盜版（的）則是pirate，和海盜的名詞一樣，也可以當形容詞使用。

7. a thorn in her flesh　眼中釘
   thorn是刺，flesh是肉；這句話就是如眼中釘、肉中刺。

8. cheongsam *n.*　旗袍
   此為長衫的發音，也可以寫作qipao。

9. come in handy　派上用場

10. carefully selected　精心挑選的

11. considerate *adj.*　貼心
    同義詞還有intimate、sweet。

12. hospitality *n.*　招待、款待

💬 練習題

- This _____ has many _____.
- You should pay more attention on the company _____.
- Thank you for your hearty _____.
- David has always seen me as _____.
- When I took a trip to Italy, my Italian finally _____.

- 這位<u>藝人</u>具有許多<u>原創</u>的作品。
- 你應該多留意公司的<u>小道消息</u>。
- 謝謝你們誠心的<u>招待</u>。
- 大衛一直視我為<u>眼中釘</u>。
- 當我去義大利旅行時，我的義大利文終於<u>派上用場</u>了。

💬 解 答

1. celebrity
2. original work
3. grapevine
4. hospitality
5. a thorn in his flesh
6. came in handy

主題 ❺ 接待國外客戶 Reception of Foreign Guests

職場補給站：以接待朋友的心態來迎接

　　不論是初入職場，或者職場老鳥，對於接待國外客戶，有些人可以説是避之惟恐不及，或者害怕自己沒有辦法扮演好其中的角色。但是反觀如果是外國人接待來訪的華人，很少人會覺得不自在；他們大多期待這一天的到來，以接待朋友的心態，以及周全的準備。

畢竟是接待文化、教育背景不同的「外國」人，所以在接待之前，有幾點基本的心態調整：

❶ 以接待朋友、家人的心態。想一想如果有位許久不見的朋友或親戚，遠道而來，我們會做足哪些準備？首先想必是一間舒適的旅館可以好好休息，當地有特色的餐館可以品嘗風味餐飲，一些有助瞭解當地風土民情的旅遊景點，甚至加上一些最近流行的庶民文化體驗行程……等等。

❷ 不用太過熱情也不把對方當成陌生人。即便是第一次見面，也要避免將對方當成陌生人來接待，可以事先擬定一些話題，諸如：彼此國家的體育、飲食習慣、菜餚、休閒方式……等等，都有助縮短距離。此外，也不必刻意熱情接待，否則反而弄巧成拙。對於接待幾次的外國客人，倒是可以安排一些近距離與接待方家庭成員互動的行程，在談公事以外將對方視作家人款待，相信可以增添彼此的信任。

接下來説説比較具體的建議：

❶ 咖啡扮演重要角色。根據多年的觀察，咖啡無論對任何國家的人，都有很大的緩和作用，如果會議是在上午或者剛過中午舉行，新鮮的咖啡（非三合一即溶）對現場氣氛的緩和有很大作用；大部分國外客人（台灣人也是）對於現場有提供咖啡、小點心的話，心情會顯得比較愉悦，有助於商

務洽談事項的進行。對英國客人的話,記得多準備一項—紅茶。

❷ 勿忘小細節。準備迎接客人到來之前,有許多公事上的資料要準備,可能會遺忘某些也相當重要的細節。舉例來說,用餐時是不是有人有不同飲食習慣,例如:不吃豬肉、不吃海鮮,甚至現場有無提供刀叉……等等,在餐廳選擇上就要事先詢問好以利訂位。知道對方的喜好也可以在送禮、行程安排上更準確地挑選。

❸ 如果時間允許,請安排一次在地的體驗之旅。假設客人的行程有半日或一日的空檔,在徵求客人同意後,可以安排一個市區或近郊的文化體驗之旅。鶯歌手燒陶、樂器博物館、手作體驗館……等等,不但可以加深客人對台灣的認識,還可以增進彼此情感。

❹ 行程務必與對方確認。不論是提前或者抵達的第一天,都要與客人溝通接下來的行程,才不會讓客人無所適從。當然,也會遇到客人想要調整某些行程的情況,最好的方式就是提醒對方,因為交通工具要事先安排,如果要調動行程,最好提前一至兩天提出來;對接待方來說,也多了調度的時間。

Part
Six

安排上司行程
Arrange Boss's Schedules

Unit 01

行程確認
Schedule Confirmation

對話 1 Conversation 1

Karl	Good morning, Melanie. I would like to confirm today's schedule with you.	早安，美拉妮。我想和您確認一下今天的行程。
Melanie	Go ahead.	說吧。
Karl	There is a con-call with German clients at ten O'clock. ①	上午10點有個與德國客戶的電話會議。
Melanie	OK, just remind me ending it as soon as possible. I remember that we have to go to the hotel where the new product launch is held at eleven thirty. ②	好的，提醒我要盡快結束。我記得11點半我們必須出發去新品發表會的飯店。
Karl	Yes. They prepare lunch at the hotel.	是的。他們在飯店準備有午餐。
Melanie	Please give me a sandwich and coffee, and don't forget that I am Ovo-Lacto Vegetarian. What time does the press conference start?	午餐請準備三明治和咖啡給我，記得我吃蛋奶素。記者會幾點開始？
Karl	At 2 PM.	下午兩點。

Melanie	Wait a minute, 2 PM? Then I can end the con-call at twelve. I can go to the hotel later. ③	等等，兩點？那電話會議我可以進行到12點鐘。飯店晚點過去。
Karl	How about change to departure at 12 thirty? ④	改成12點半過去怎麼樣？
Melanie	Great. What else I need to do except making a speech?	很好。除了致詞我還需要做什麼？
Karl	Nothing. I already E-Mailed you the final edition of speech draft yesterday.	不用。昨天我已經將最後版本的演講稿E-mail給您了。⑤
Melanie	I saw it. Well done, Karl.	我看到了。做得很好，卡爾。
Karl	Thank you. After the press conference, the driver will take you to Taipei Songshan Airport. ⑥	卡爾：謝謝。記者會後，司機會送您去松山機場。
Melanie	Yes, I have to attend the Asia-Pacific Management Meeting. When is the flight?	對，上海有個亞太區主管會議必須出席。幾點的飛機？
Karl	6 PM, so it's fine you arrive the airport at four. ⑦	下午六點，所以四點到機場就可以了。
Melanie	OK, we have to leave there no late than 3 o'clock.	好的，我們最晚三點必須離開記者會場。

實用應答小撇步 1

① There is an interview at afternoon / There is a Shareholder meeting on Tuesday / Going to attend an exhibition in Hong Kong next first

下午有個記者訪問／星期二有場股東大會／下個月一號要去香港參加展覽

② Must departure before 10 / Cannot late than 3 PM / This time cannot be changed

10點前一定要出發／不能晚於下午三點／這個時間不能更改

③ You go first, I will catch up with you later / The flight is delayed / Cannot catch up with this schedule, please cancel it

你們先去，我隨後就到／飛機誤點起飛了／這個行程趕不及了，請取消它

④ Can the meeting changed to tomorrow? / Re-book the restaurant to any one near by the company / Can you change this schedule to next fifth?

改成明天開會可以嗎？／餐廳改成在公司附近的任一家／可以把這個行程改到下個月五號嗎？

⑤ He already provided you the related materials of the business trip the day before yesterday / I already scheduled this month's meetings last month / The visiting schedules in Shanghai have been confirmed by phone calls

前天他已經將出差相關的資料提供給您了／上個月我已經將本月的會議行程安排妥當／下週的上海拜訪行程都電話確認好了

⑥ We can go by taxi / The metro can arrive directly to the International Airport / It can only arrived by bus

我們搭計程車過去／地鐵可以直達國際機場／只能搭巴士前往

⑦ Just let me receive by tomorrow / It would be fine if it can be confirmed by next Wednesday

明天讓我收到就可以了／下週三以前確認好就可以了

對話 **2** Conversation **2**

Bridget	Hi, Gene. Are you available right now?	嗨，金。有空嗎？
Gene	I am a little busy right now, but I think yes. Go ahead.	有點忙，還可以。妳說吧。
Bridget	Boss is going to a business trip this week, and I already booked the tickets and hotel.	老闆這週要出差，機票和酒店我已經訂好了。
Gene	OK, hand them to me. I will go with him. ①	好的，交給我吧。我會陪老闆一起去。
Bridget	I booked yours, too.	妳的我也訂好了。
Gene	Thanks.	謝謝妳啦。
Bridget	You are welcome. The American clients will visit us after boss comes back.	不客氣。老闆回來後接著美國客人會來訪。
Gene	I am afraid the fight will delay, could you set the visiting back one day? ②	我怕飛機會延誤，可不可以把客人來訪時間延後一天呢？
Bridget	I will try to talk with them. What if they don't agree? ③	我會去溝通看看，萬一不行怎麼辦？
Gene	Then insert a city sightseeing tour, please. ④	那麼就麻煩妳安插市區觀光行程吧。

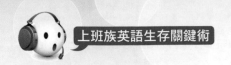

Bridget	All right, I will be resourceful.	好的，我會隨機應變。
Gene	Thank you.	感謝妳。
Bridget	And, Boss has a TV interview on the third day when the clients are still here. ⑤	對了，客人還在的第三天，老闆有個電視專訪。
Gene	We need a rehearsal before the interview, so ask the TV station if they can send someone over before the day. ⑥⑦	受訪前需要彩排，問問電視台可否在前一天派人過來？
Bridget	Usually it's prepared before the few hours on that day, so it would be difficult to set it before the day.	通常是當天的幾個小時前做準備，前一天可能有困難。
Gene	Sounds reasonable.	也對。
Bridget	I'd better be going busy if there is no question. Wish you a safe journey.	沒問題的話，我就去忙了。祝妳一路順風。

實用應答小撇步 2

① Will you go with me? / Will he attend this meeting? / How many people are going to join together?

妳會和我一起去嗎？／他也要出席這個會議嗎？／有多少人要一起參加？

② Cannot this schedule be advanced by two hours? / The date of my arriving at Taiwan will be postponed / He wishes this event can be held on time

不能將這個行程提前兩小時嗎？／我會延後回來台灣／他希望這個活動準時舉行

③ What if she says no? / What if he turns down (says yes)? / What we should do if the clients delayed?

萬一她說不行呢？／如果他拒絕（同意）呢？／客戶遲到的話，我們該怎麼辦？

④ Please exchange these two schedules / I would like to re-put schedule A in front of B / Please move this schedule to after 3 PM

請你替換這兩個行程／我想將A行程改排在B行程之前／把這個行程移到下午三點以後

⑤ General Manager has a magazine interview at afternoon / there is a radio interview tomorrow morning / There is an opening ribbon-cutting ceremony the day after tomorrow

總經理下午有個雜誌專訪／明天上午有個電台訪問／後天有一個開幕剪綵儀式

⑥ Need to practice before the presentation / Need to simulate the negotiation

簡報前需要演練一下／談判需要模擬一下

⑦ Can it be proceed tomorrow? / Can it be held at next week?

能不能在明天進行？／可否在下週舉辦？

單字與句型

1. con-call *n.* 電話會議
   全寫為conference call。

2. new product launch 新產品上市發表會
   launch也可做動詞使用，所以發表新品就寫作launch new product。

3. Lacto Vegetarian 蛋奶素食主義者
   全寫為Lacto-ovo-vegetarian Diet；Lacto是拉丁文lactis的變化形，葡萄牙文裡牛奶(milk)的意思，ovo則是葡萄牙文（也是源於拉丁文）裡雞蛋的意思。全素（不食肉、魚、蛋及乳製品）為Vegan Diet。

4. press conference 記者會

6. departure *n.* 出發
   在機場也經常看到這個單詞，相反詞為arrive，抵達。

   departure terminal 出發航廈

   departing /arriving flights 出發／抵達航班

7. catch up with 趕上
   用以形容在課業、距離、速度上趕上其他人。

8. set back 往後延
   相同用法有：postpone、put off。

   The meeting was put off until next week. 會議延到了下週。

   The flight is postponed for an hour. 飛機往後延了一個小時。

9. resourceful *adj.* 隨機應變的、足智多謀的

10. advanced by 被提前
    相同用法有：in advance、bring forward。

    Reservations can be made up to 2 hours in advance of the departure. 出發兩小時前可以預約。

    They decided to bring forward the date of the meeting. 他們決定將會議的日期提前。

練習題

A: Do you know when the boss should _____ the _____?

B: 3 PM.

A: So, he should _____ at 2?

B: Sort of.

A: Should we cancel the _____ meeting at one thirty?

B: No. _____ to 10.

A: What about the presentation meeting at 10?

B: _____ until come back from the conference.

A：你知道老闆幾點要出席記者會？

B：下午三點。

A：所以兩點就要出發了？

B：差不多。

A：一點半的電話會議要幫他取消嗎？

B：不用。提前到10點吧。

A：那10點的簡報會議呢？

B：延後到記者會回來吧。

解 答

1. attend

2. press conference

3. departure

4. con-call

5. Bring forward

6. Postpone / Put off

Unit 02 訂位 Booking

對話 1 Conversation 1

Gabriel	Hello, Ella. I want to know if you booked the tickets and hotels for the oversea trips from next Friday.	喂，艾拉。我想知道下週五開始的國外行程，機票和酒店訂好了嗎？
Ella	Yes, Boss. They are all booked.	是，老闆。都訂好了。
Gabriel	You know I don't like a window seat during a long flight, [1] so is it an aisle seat? [2]	妳知道長途飛行我不喜歡靠窗，飛機座位是不是靠走道？
Ella	I am sorry, Boss, I forgot that. I will change it immediately later.	糟糕，老闆，我忘了。等一下馬上改好。
Gabriel	All right. Did you book a non-smoking floor at the hotel? [3]	好吧。還有酒店是不是訂了非吸菸樓層？
Ella	Yes, I didn't forget that.	是的，這個我沒忘記。
Gabriel	Very good. Moreover, there is no return date on the ticket, is it? [4]	很好。還有，機票回程沒有打上日期吧？
Ella	No, as you required, I asked the travel agency to make it open return.	沒有的，就是照您說的，我請旅行社開不指定日期。

Gabriel	Good. Because my return date is depending on the schedule, I cannot sure right now.	很好。我回來的時間依行程而定，現在也不確定。
Ella	I understand.	了解。
Gabriel	By the way, where are the movie tickets for tonight?	對了，今天晚上的電影票呢？
Ella	The seats are booked, Boss. They are the middle seats in the back row. ⑤	訂好位子了，老闆。後排的中間座位。
Gabriel	Very good, thanks. Just give them to me.	很好，謝謝。給我吧。
Ella	But, Boss, since they are fully booked tonight, so there is one person must seat at the right corner at the front. ⑥	但是，老闆，晚上客滿，所以有一個人要坐到前面的右手邊角落。
Gabriel	Oh, that's really terrible. Then please return the tickets, and check if there is any good seat from other movies. ⑦	喔，這真是糟糕。那就退掉吧，看看另外一部有沒有好的座位。
Ella	I'll check it right now.	我馬上替您查。

實用應答小撇步 1

① I like to seat behind my favorite team's dugout when I watch a baseball game / He likes a restaurant where serves local cuisine / Do you prefer a window or aisle seat?

我喜歡看棒球賽時坐在我喜歡的球隊的休息區後方／他喜歡供應當地風味餐的餐廳／你喜歡靠窗還是靠走道的位子？

② Is it the best place seats? / Is it at stage (smoking / non-smoking) area? / I need a seat for physically disabled

是不是視線最好的位子？／是不是舞台（吸菸／非吸菸）區？／我需要一個肢障者的位子

③ Did you order a vegetarian meal for lunch? / Did he order a table for ten at the restaurant?

午餐妳是不是有訂了一份素食餐點？／他是不是向餐廳預訂了十人的座位？

④ Doesn't this group buying movie ticket specify date? / Does this coupon have any deadline for using?

這張團購電影票沒有指定使用日期吧？／這張優惠券是限期使用嗎？

⑤ The third seat from the right / The seat in the middle row by the aisle / The seat in the second row middle from the front (top)

右邊數來第三個座位／中間排靠走道的位置／前（上）面數來第二排中間的位子

⑥ Have to move to the next table / Change seat with the front row / Need to share a table with other customers

要移動到隔壁桌／要和前排的人換座位／要和其他客人併桌

⑦ Then change the date / Then I would like to pay more for it / We ask for a refund

那就改期吧／那我願意多付點錢／我們要求退錢

對話 2 Conversation 2

Enoch	Hi, Francis, how's everything going?	弗蘭西斯，最近好嗎？ 很好啊，你呢？
Francis	Great. You?	
Enoch	Thanks for asking, I am doing OK. By the way, the company is going to have a celebratory dinner [①] and we need to find a restaurant for one hundred people. [②]	多謝問候，還可以。對了，公司要辦慶功宴，需要找一間容納一百人的餐廳。
Francis	It's easy. What about the style of the restaurant?	這不難。餐廳風格呢？
Enoch	Well, not too serious, can allow some activities.	嗯，不要太嚴肅的，可以辦一些活動的。
Francis	Got you. I suggest a Mexican or Spanish restaurant, you can even dance Salsa. [③]	了解。我建議墨西哥或者西班牙餐廳吧。還可以跳騷莎舞。
Enoch	Right, speak of which, we need to hire a band except dancing.	對了，講到活動。除了跳舞，還要請一些樂隊表演。
Francis	OK, I'll make sure they play some passionate music.	好的，那我讓他們演奏熱情一點的音樂吧。
Enoch	Great, thanks. And, some people don't eat meat, can they prepare	很棒，謝謝。還有，有人不吃肉，可以準備一些海

	more seafood and vegetable? ④	鮮或者蔬菜？
Francis	It should be fine if we book one week earlier.	提前一週訂位都沒問題的。
Enoch	What about liquor? Should we also prepare more?	酒精飲料呢？要不要也多準備一些？
Francis	Of course, it's a celebratory party!	當然，是慶功宴！
Enoch	Don't drink and drive, but remember let the restaurant help to call taxies for you.	酒後不開車，記得讓餐廳幫你們叫計程車啊。
Francis	Don't worry. The foreman will help, isn't it?	別擔心。領班會幫忙的，對吧？
Enoch	Should be fine. Just reminding, you must pay a 10% deposit when you make the booking. ⑥	應該沒問題。提醒一下，訂位要先付10%的訂金。
Enoch	Can you pay for me first?	可以請你先墊嗎？
Francis	Don't kidding with me. It's your company's event!	別開玩笑了，這可是你們公司的活動呀！

實用應答小撇步 2

① The company's ten-year anniversary will be holding at Taipei Arena / General Manager wants to reward the Sales Department

公司10周年慶活動將在台北小巨蛋舉行／總經理要獎勵業務部門

② Want to book the venue for press conference for two hours / Want to rent the tourist buses for company trip for four nights and five days / Want to plan an annual staff travel

要訂兩小時的記者會場地／要租五天四夜公司旅遊的遊覽車／要規劃一年一度的員工旅遊

③ This restaurant is famous for Mediterranean dishes / I suggest we go to the movie theater that famous for providing latest 4D movies / Which theater you suggest us to go to?

這間餐廳以地中海風味菜聞名／我建議我們去以提供最新**4D**電影聞名的電影院／你建議我們去看哪一齣舞台劇？

④ Does anyone have an allergy to seafood? / Please prepare Multinational cuisine / Buffet service style allows everyone to choice the dishes they like

有人對海鮮過敏嗎？／請準備多國料理／自助式可以讓大家自由選擇自己喜歡的菜

⑤ Pay the deposit when you book / The deposit will be confiscated if cancel the reservation

預約就要付押金／取消預約就會被沒收訂金

⑥ Can I ask for an advance? / Can the company pay for it? / Can it be borrowed from you?

我可以要求預支嗎？／可以由公司買單嗎？／可以向你先借嗎？

💬 單字與句型

1. window seat / aisle seat　靠窗／靠走道的位子
2. as you required　如您要求的
   I enclose a copy of our company profile as you required.　如您所要求的，我隨信附上一份我司的公司簡介。
3. open return　不指定回程日期
   也可以寫成open-ended。

   Hi, I would like to book an open-ended airline ticket to Shanghai.　嗨，我想要訂一張去上海且不指定回程日期的機票。
4. depend on...　由…決定、依…而定
   A: Will you attend the party tonight?　妳會出席今晚的派對嗎？
   B: Well, it depends.　嗯，看情況囉。
   depend on 還有信賴、依靠(count on)的意思。
   You can depend on his honesty.　你可以信賴他說的話。
5. physically disabled　肢障者
   這個詞由兩個單詞組成，physically是身體上地意思，disabled是無法起作用的意思。兩者合一，意思就是肢體障礙者的意思。
6. group buying　團購的
7. coupon *n.*　優惠券、折價券
8. refund *v.*　退費
9. speak of which　提到這個、說到這
   相似用法有：Speak of the devil, the devil appears，說曹操，曹操到的意思。
10. foreman *n.*　領班
    工地的工頭、陪審長也用這個字。
11. an allergy to seafood　對海鮮過敏
12. Buffet service style　自助式
13. confiscate *v.*　沒收

💬 練習題

- She has _____.
- May I have an _____ seat, please?
- This is a _____.
- I complained to _____, but he ignored me.
- His return ticket is _____.

- 她對牛肉過敏。
- 麻煩你，給我一個靠走道的位子。
- 這是團購的折價券。
- 我向領班抱怨過，但是他不理我。
- 他的回程機票沒有指定日期。

💬 解　答

1. an allergy to beef
2. aisle
3. group buying
4. coupon
5. foreman
6. open return / open-ended

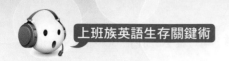
Unit 03 改行程 Changing Schedules

對話 1 Conversation 1

Phil	Livia, Boss just canceled the business trip next week.①
	莉維亞，老闆剛才把下週的出差都取消了。
Livia	OK. So, can the next two weeks' schedules be advanced by the next week?
	好的。那麼下下週的行程是不是可以提前安排到下週呢？
Phil	Such as?
	例如哪些行程？
Livia	Vivian from T TV Station would like to arrange the exclusive interview ASAP. ②
	T電視台的記者薇薇安希望盡早安排獨家專訪。
Phil	Let me discuss with Boss, I am afraid that we haven't got all the materials ready. ③
	讓我和老闆討論一下，我怕資料沒有準備齊全。
Livia	Sure.
	沒問題。
Phil	Anything else?
	還有嗎？
Livia	Yes. The General Manager of C Company also wishes to meet with Boss ASAP.
	有的。C公司的總經理也希望盡早和老闆會面。
Phil	I need to ask Boss first. ④ Did he
	這個我需要先詢問老闆。

	mention the things to discuss about?	他有說要談什麼？
Livia	Boss only asked me to arrange the meetings, didn't mention the contents. Besides, it's always you to be with Boss at the meeting.	老闆只有請我安排會議，沒有提到內容。而且一向是你陪同老闆參加會議的。
Phil	Right, thanks for reminding. What else of them need to shift? ⑤	對的，謝謝提醒。還有哪些要移動的嗎？
Livia	So, Boss can attend the Manager Meeting next week, cannot he?	所以下週的公司主管會議，老闆就可以出席了，對吧？
Phil	Yes, he can, please arrange into daily schedules. ⑥	是的，請排進行程裡。
Livia	No problem. That's all.	沒問題。就這些了。
Phil	OK. Should we go to lunch together later?	好的。等會兒一起吃午餐？
Livia	I have an appointment with a friend. Something came up to her yesterday, so we rescheduled for today. ⑦	我約了朋友，她昨天臨時有事，改到今天。

實用應答小撇步 ❶

① Tomorrow's flights are canceled because of a typhoon / The meeting at the day after tomorrow needs to postpone to next Monday / Do we need to advance the manager meeting?

明天的班機因為颱風取消了／後天的會議需要推遲到下週一／我們需要將主管會議提前舉行嗎？

② She wishes the sooner this schedule can be confirmed, the better / I wish the sooner I can book the tickets, the better / It's fine to set this meeting on Friday 她希望越早確定行程越好／我希望越快訂到機票越好／這個會議排在週五也沒關係

③ Let me talk to my client / Please confirm with the Supervisor

讓我與客戶溝通一下／請你與主管確認一下

④ I need to consult with my supervisor / Let him make few calls to ask / Do you need to confirm with the manager?

這件事我需要諮詢我的主管／讓他先打幾通電話詢問一下／你需要和上司確認嗎？

⑤ What else among the meetings need to adjust the contents of discussion? / Please revise the list of attending media of this press conference / Change to invite client A to attend this meeting together

還有哪些會議要修改討論內容的？／請修改這次記者會邀請出席的媒體名單／這個會議改邀請A客戶一起出席

⑥ Please delete from the schedule / Please shift this discussion after next meeting 請從行程裡刪除／請移到下次會議後再討論

⑦ He took a sick leave yesterday, so postpone for today / I had personal leave last week so I couldn't attend / Won't you have something just came up, will you?

他昨天生病，所以延到今天／我上週請事假，所以不能出席／你不會臨時有事不能來吧？

對話 **2** Conversation **2**

Patti	Hi, Boss.	嗨,老闆。
Ruth	What is it?	什麼事?
Patti	Here's your schedule for next week. Please let me know if you have any question. ①	這是您下週的行程,如果有任何疑問,請讓我知道。
Ruth	Thank you.	謝謝。
Patti	You are welcome. But, Boss, the international flights are all cancelled due to the typhoon in Hong Kong. ②	不客氣。不過,老闆,香港因為颱風的關係,國際航班全部停飛。
Ruth	What?	什麼?
Patti	I am afraid that we need to change the flight. ③ Flight to Tokyo first, and then transfer to London. ④ What do you think?	恐怕我們要更改航班了。先飛到東京,再轉機到倫敦。您看怎麼樣?
Ruth	Good, Patti. Let's do this.	很好,帕蒂。就這麼辦。
Patti	And, Boss, what return date do you prefer? ⑤	還有,老闆,返程日期您希望是哪一天?
Ruth	December, seventh.	12月7日。
Patti	Sure, no problem. Besides that, I need to arrange the Annual	好的,沒有問題。另外,我要安排年度股東會議,

	Meeting of Stockholders. How long do you think it will take? ⑥	您估計需要多少時間？
Ruth	The whole afternoon, I guess.	一整個下午吧，我猜。
Patti	OK, if so, we need to change the time of the meeting with Sales Department.	好的，如果是這樣的話，下午和業務部門的會議就要改時間了。
Ruth	Change to some other day.	改到隔天吧。
Patti	No problem. By the way, your wedding anniversary is tonight and the restaurant is booked.	沒問題。對了，晚上是您結婚周年紀念日，餐廳已經訂好了。
Ruth	Please tell the driver, take the devious route to dry cleaning shop after departure from the office. ⑦	請轉告司機，從公司出發後先繞道載我去乾洗店。
Patti	Got you. I should get busy, then.	知道了。那我先去忙了。

實用應答小撇步 **2**

① If you have any further question, please feel free to contact me / Please feel free to call me and I will continually provide full support

如有進一步疑問,請隨時聯繫我/請隨時聯繫我,我將提供持續地協助

② The High-Speed Rail stops running for one hour / Taiwan Railways canceled ten trains

高鐵停駛一小時/台鐵取消十個班次

③ I am afraid that we have to change the meeting agenda / I am afraid that we need to change the routes

恐怕我們要更改會議大綱了/恐怕我們要更改路線了

④ Discuss topic B first, then back to A / Go back to the hotel, then to the office / Have a con-call with foreign clients this morning, followed by one hour interview

先討論B議題,再回頭討論A議題/先回飯店,再去辦公室/今天早上先和國外客戶電話會議,接著有一小時面試

⑤ What date do you prefer to change the meeting to? / When does he wish to visit? / I hope do not change the date

您希望將會議改到哪一天?/他希望何時來訪?/我希望不要改期

⑥ How long will it take (do we need to wait)? / Should we wait forever? / How much longer will it take before the ending?

要等多久?/我們該一直等下去嗎?/還有多久結束?

⑦ Please drive me to the office in passing / Skipping lunch, let's go to visit our clients directly

請順便載我去辦公室/略過午餐,我們直接拜訪客戶吧!

💬 單字與句型

1. exclusive interview　獨家採訪
   I saw an exclusive interview with Bill Gates last night.　昨晚我看了一個比爾蓋茲的獨家專訪。

2. shift *v.*　移動、交換
   也有輪班、調動、替換的意思。
   A sudden shift in the wind warned of the coming storm.　風向的突然轉變警告即將到來的一場風暴。

3. consult *v.*　諮詢
   名詞是consultancy。另外有一個相似的名詞，consultant是顧問的意思。
   She is my consultant in my career.　她是我生涯規劃的顧問。

4. sick leave / personal leave　病假／事假
   各種請假的說法：
   maternity leave產假、paternity leave陪產假、official leave公假、merriage leave婚假、funeral leave喪假、annual leave年假／特休。

5. take the devious route　繞道
   也可以寫成take a detour或make a detour。
   This evening, there were a lot of traffic jams so I took a detour home.
   今天晚上大塞車，所以我繞道回家了。

6. continually *adv.*　不間斷地、持續地

7. meeting agenda　會議大綱

8. followed by...　接著、接下來是…
   "No" is always followed by a negative answer, and "Yes" is followed by a positive answer.　「不」後面總是接著一個否定的答案，「是」後面則是接著肯定的答案。

9. in passing　順便

💬 練習題

- I _____ Boss his opinion about last time's _____.
- I mention this point now _____ and shall refer to it again.
- I will have _____ tomorrow.

- 我諮詢了老闆對上次獨家專訪的意見。
- 我順便提及這點，待會應該還會提到。
- 明天我請事假。

💬 解 答

1. consulted
2. exclusive interview
3. in passing
4. personal leave

主題 ❻ 安排上司行程 Arrange Boss's Schedules

職場補給站：讓上司也能「乖乖聽你的」

　　多數人可能沒有想過，安排上司行程的人，換個角度來說，其實是上司的「老闆」。如果朝這個方向思考和行事的話，安排行程就不是一件無聊、枯燥的工作，而是掌握了許多形勢走向，需要格外謹慎與細心(needs more cautious and careful)。

　　曾經有人說過，離權力核心越近，嘴巴越緊，這句話說得可一點兒沒有錯。美國影集「紙牌屋(House of Cards)」裡，男主角就曾經告誡過身邊的保鑣兼司機：「從現在起，你就是一顆石頭；你聽不見、看不見，更不會對別人對我的質疑起疑心。」這句話或許也可以成為安排上司行程的工作者的教條之一。

　　不論上司的對象是本國、外國人，都有下列幾項建議給安排上司行程的職場人：

❶ 牢記上司的習慣(keep Boss's habits in mind)。這點很重要，記性是這個工作的第一要件(the first requirement in this job)；但是即使工作多年的人也會發現，有時候手上事情太多的話，記不住也會變成家常便飯，所以利用紀錄就是唯一解決之道。

❷ 將上司擺在首位(Boss should be put in the first place)。這是相對於對方而言，因為有時候對方的職銜(title)比自己的上司還大時，也得要顧及自己長官的地位、面子，所以在溝通的當下，永遠要記得自己的上司是誰，不需要事事遷就對方，刻意矮化自己的上司。

❸ 對行程保密(keep the schedule secret)。這個在職場上是有技巧的，因為無論對方是誰，都不必要直接透漏上司的行蹤，否則有心人可以事後追蹤，會落得露出馬腳(show the cloven foot)的下場。所以可以委婉地説：「現在會議中，不方便接聽電話／接見。請留下聯繫方式，我們會盡速與您聯繫。(He / She is now at a meeting, please leave a message or contact information and we will contact you as soon as possible.)」

❹ 想在老闆之前並且預測某些事情(think ahead and anticipate)。此技巧和第一點的記性相呼應，因為長久相處下來的習慣，知道老闆的喜好、厭惡，所以能想在老闆之前，甚至，有時候老闆會忘記之前他的指示而做出矛盾的行程指揮，這時候就要提醒老闆衝突的行程，由上司定奪哪一個行程比較要緊(which one is more important)。預測某些事情則是指，因為知道老闆身邊的人如何互動，有時候可以適時提醒一下老闆，如果這個行程排進去或者修改了，可能造成哪些事情也會跟著異動。

　　許多職場技巧或者心得，絕非一蹴可幾、一夜可成，需要時間的累積才能有好的成果展現出來。就連看似沒有甚麼技巧的安排行程，其實也隱藏著魔鬼細節(The devil is in the details)；畢竟掌握行蹤的人至關重要，所以有些秘書或者司機，在勝任之前甚至需要經過身家調查，就是這個原因。

Part
Seven

突發狀況
Unexpected Situations

Unit 01 有人示威抗議 Protests

對話 1 Conversation 1

Irving	Congratulations, Tina. You have already gone to two days of the orientation training session.	恭喜妳，媞娜。已經上過新人訓練兩天課程了。
Tina	Today is the last day, isn't it? What are we going to do?	今天是最後一天了吧。我們準備上些什麼呢？
Irving	We are going to talk about meeting an emergency.	是遇到突發狀況時的應變。
Tina	This issue probably is a little difficult for me.	這個議題對我來説可能難了些。
Irving	Don't worry, we take step by step.① First, when company security inform you unexpected situation has happened, you have to make a judgment.	別緊張，一步一步來。首先，當公司警衛通知妳有突發狀況時，妳要先判斷。
Tina	Make a judgment about what?	判斷什麼呢？
Irving	About what kind of unexpected situation it is. For example, is it a peaceful or a violent protest? Some of them even bring media directly.	判斷是哪一類的突發事件。舉例來説，有平和的示威抗議、或激烈的，也有直接帶媒體記者來的。

Tina	What should I do if it is a peaceful protest? [2]	假設是平和的示威抗議，我該怎麼做？
Irving	Listen to their comments or demands with company security. [3] If they want to deliver a petition, accept it and then in care of company executives. [4]	和公司警衛一起，聽取他們的意見或訴求。如果有陳情書，接過來，轉交給公司高層就可以了。
Tina	Got you. What if there is a violent protest?	懂了。如果遇到激烈的抗議呢？
Irving	Then you should call the police and hand it over to them. Ask the people to leave, because here is workplace and we don't want our colleagues get hurt. [5]	那麼就要報警，交由警察處理。請他們離開公司，因為這裡是辦公場所，我們也不希望同事受傷。
Tina	That sounds reasonable. But I wish this will not happen to me. [6]	聽起來很有道理。不過我希望不會遇到這種事情。
Irving	It's hard to say. We met one last year.	很難說喔。去年我們就發生了一件。
Tina	Oh My God, hope everyone was safe. [7] So, what should I do if they bring media directly?	天啊，希望人員都平安。如果是直接帶媒體來的抗議，我該怎麼做呢？
Irving	This is more complex, but basically, it combines the two of what we mentioned before. Let's exercise this afternoon.	這個就比較複雜了，但是基本上是綜合前面兩者。下午我們演練一遍吧。
Tina	Great, that's what I was going to say.	太好了，我正想這麼說呢。

實用應答小撇步　1

① Take your time / Don't you worry

慢慢來／你儘管放心

② What can we do? / We will work it out / It can't be helped

該怎麼辦？／我們總會有辦法的／沒辦法了

③ Listen carefully to the requirement of other side / Ask them to completely express their demands / Listen carefully and provide care

仔細聆聽對方需求／請他們完整表達訴求／專心聆聽與提供關懷

④ Please in care of Police (insurance company) / Forward to Chairman

請轉交給警方（保險公司）處理／轉達給董事長

⑤ Please leave quietly / Please ask them to disband as soon as possible / Ask them do not disturb other people

請你們安靜地離開／請他們盡速解散／請他們不要打擾其他人

⑥ It's bad to meet this kind of thing / Do you wish it happen?

真倒楣遇到這種事情／你希望這種事情發生嗎？

⑦ Hope everyone stays safe through this awful day / Hope no one gets hurt / Does anybody hurt?

希望所有人平安度過這糟糕的一天／希望沒有人受傷／有人受傷嗎？

對話 2 | Conversation 2

Fiona	Is everything unchanged this afternoon, General Manager? ①	總經理，下午的行程一切不變嗎？
Benjamin	I am afraid that they have to be canceled, Fiona.	恐怕得取消了，費歐娜。
Fiona	Would you mind if I ask what's going on?	您介意我問怎麼了嗎？
Benjamin	It didn't go well with talking to union representatives just now, they may organize a protest tomorrow. ②	剛才和工會代表們談得不太順利，他們明天可能會組織一場示威抗議。
Fiona	My goodness, what's the content of the protest? ③	我的天，抗議的內容是什麼呢？
Benjamin	They hope a 3% salary increase.	他們希望加薪3%。
Fiona	I just remember that we have no salary increase in many years, General Manager. ④	我想起來我們好多年沒有調薪了，總經理。
Benjamin	This has to be approved by the Board of directors.	這個事情也要董事會同意才行。
Fiona	You could try to communicate with the Board before tomorrow's protest. ⑤	您可以趕在明天示威之前和董事會溝通看看。
Benjamin	This is a good idea, Fiona.	這是個好建議，費歐娜。

Fiona	Although the result is not guaranteed, you tried your best.	雖然不保證結果，但是至少您努力了。
Benjamin	Hope the union representatives would understand. ⑥	希望工會代表們可以理解。
Fiona	I can call the police station to file a report now, just save for a rainy day. ⑦	我現在就先打電話給警察局備案，以備不時之需。
Benjamin	Jesus, Fiona, please don't scare me.	老天，費歐娜，妳可別嚇我。
Fiona	It's company administrative process, General Manager. ⑧	總經理，這是既定的公司流程。
Benjamin	All right, whatever you say. I will try my best to talk with the Board, really hope we can have a satisfied result.	好吧，就聽妳的。董事會我盡量溝通，希望有個滿意的答案。
Fiona	I think everyone is expected even if a 1% of salary increases.	我想大家希望調薪1%也好。
Benjamin	I will see what I can do.	我盡力吧。

實用應答小撇步 2

① Business as usual / Nothing has changed / You are still the same

一切照舊／一點兒也沒變／妳還是老樣子

② There might be a protest outside the annual general meeting tomorrow / There was an environmental group made a protest in front of the Company yesterday

明天的股東大會外面可能會有人示威抗議／昨天環保團體來公司前面抗議

③ Why they make a protest against our company? / What are the demands of the march? / Who joined the protest?

他們為什麼要針對我們公司進行抗議？／遊行的訴求是什麼？／哪些人參加了示威抗議？

④ The company has not adjust employee welfare for a long time / The recent layoffs are too often

公司福利好久沒有調整了／最近裁員太頻繁了

⑤ Please ask the Police to arrive at the scene before the protest / Please leave quietly after protesting / Please talk with the organizer again before the protest

請趕在示威抗議之前請警察到場／請在示威抗議之後安靜地離開／請在示威抗議之前再次和主辦單位溝通

⑥ Hope the demonstrators express demands peacefully / Hope protest representatives could accept negotiations / Hope company executives could give respond ASAP

希望示威隊伍可以平和表達訴求／希望抗議代表們可以接受談判／希望公司高層可以盡快給予回覆

⑦ Call company executives and report the situation / Call demonstrations to cancel the protest

打電話給公司高層回報狀況／打電話給抗議代表取消示威遊行

⑧ It's company rule / It has been set for years

這是公司規定／這是好早以前就定下來的

單字與句型

1. orientation training session　新人訓練課程
   orientation 是方針、嚮導的意思。

2. meeting an emergency　應變、應付緊急狀況

3. make a judgment　判斷
   To make a judgment is to draw a conclusion or make a decision about something.　做出判斷就是對某事做出結論或做決定。

4. in care of　轉交給某人
   Please in care of Miss Chen.　請轉交給陳小姐。

   國際貿易上還有一種簡寫方式：C/O，其實就是care of的縮寫。

5. disband *v.*　解散

6. disturb *v.*　打擾
   Do I disturb you?　我打擾到你了嗎？

7. awful *adj.*　糟糕的
   同義詞有terrible、bad。

   How awful is it?　（情況）有多糟糕？

8. environmental group　環保團體

9. march *n.*　示威遊行
   也寫作demonstration；示威抗議的人則是demonstrator。

   Thousands of people are demonstrating outside the factory.　工廠外面有成千上萬的民眾在示威。

10. employee welfare　員工福利
    也可以寫作employee benefits。

11. layoff *n.*　裁員
    當作動詞使用時為lay off，還有停止、關閉、停歇的意思。

    I've smoked cigarettes for years, but now I'm going to lay off them.
    我抽菸好幾年了，但是現在我即將要戒掉它們。

💬 練習題

- Please do not _____ me again when I am taking a rest.
- Our _____ is pretty _____.
- The subject of this time's _____ is how to _____.
- This is from Mr. Chen _____ Mr. Wang.

- 請不要再打擾我休息。
- 我們的員工福利挺糟糕的。
- 這次新人訓練課程主題是如何應付緊急狀況。
- 這是陳先生要轉交給王先生的。

💬 解　答

1. disturb
2. employee welfare
3. awful
4. orientation training session
5. meet an emergency
6. in care of

Unit 02 發生火災地震 Fire and Earthquake

對話 1 | Conversation 1

Vic	Hilda, how's everything? What's your schedule this week?	熙爾妲，怎麼樣，妳這週有什麼行程嗎？
Hilda	Hi, Manager. I am going to share the information of fire training and courses with colleagues tomorrow.	是的，主管。明天要和同仁分享火災訓練課程內容。
Vic	Right, I remember you went to the class last week, didn't you? Can you share with me now?	對了，我記得妳是上週去上課的。妳可以先和我分享嗎？
Hilda	Of course. First, make sure that inflammable items are stored in sealed containers. [1]	當然可以。首先，易燃物品應該收在密封的容器裡。
Vic	This rule is also suitable when at home. I think I'm going to keep the lighter in my drawer later.	這在家裡也適用呢。我想等下就要把我的打火機收在抽屜裡。
Hilda	Sure, Manager.	對呀，主管。
Vic	So, what else we can do for preventing fire? [2]	還有哪些動作可以預防火災？
Hilda	The Company should have wiring	公司應該經常請電工檢查

	often examined by electricians, to prevent fire. [3]	線路，以防止火災。
Vic	Is that so? Then I should inform Administration Division to deal with it. [4]	這樣啊，那我應該通知管理部門去處理。
Hilda	One more, this is more suitable for factories. That is keeping working environment well-ventilated anytime. [5]	還有一點，適用在工廠。就是要隨時保持工作環境通風。
Vic	It is easy to understand. There will be too much carbon monoxide and carbon dioxide in a poorly ventilated area.	這很容易理解，因為不通風就會有過多的二氧化碳或一氧化碳。
Hilda	I guess so.	我想是吧。
Vic	So, what we should do if there is fire occur?	萬一遇到火災，該怎麼辦？
Hilda	First, calm down and do not get panic. Crawl down on the floor and move to the opposite direction from the fire followed by escape routes. [6]	首先冷靜，勿驚慌。按照逃生路線，盡量靠近地面，往火災的反方向離開。
Vic	Wow, you sound professional.	哇，妳真的很專業。
Hilda	Last but not least, call for help and wait for professional help. [7] Don't go back inside for any reason, and that's all.	最後，打電話求救並等待專業的協助到達，無論如何，不回到火場。這樣就好囉。

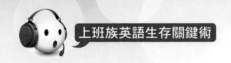

實用應答小撇步 1

① Fire extinguishers should be located in its designated place / First aid kit should be kept in a public place

滅火器應該放在指定的地方／急救醫藥箱應該放在公用區域

② What are other disaster prevention steps? / What are other contingency plans?

還有哪些災害預防步驟？／還有哪些緊急應變措施？

③ Disaster prevent and rescue exercise is held regularly / Routine fire extinguisher inspection / we are bound to have safety check of buildings often examined by technicians

固定舉辦災害防救演習／每月例行檢查滅火器／經常請技術進行建築物公安檢查

④ Inform Administration Department to announce to everyone / Inform Accounting Department to pay / Inform General Manager come to attend

通知行政部門公告給大家／通知會計部門去付款／通知總經理來參加

⑤ Keep vigilant at all times / Keep walkway clear at all times / Hold emergency preparedness exercises regularly

隨時保持警覺／隨時保持走道暢通／定期做防災演習

⑥ To exit to the entrance of the building / Go to the roof and wait for the rescue / To escape by using an emergency ladder

往大樓的門口疏散／到樓頂等待救援／利用緊急避難梯逃生

⑦ Call family to confirm safety / Call General Manager and report the progress in disaster relief

打電話給親人報平安／打電話給總經理回報救災進度

對話 2 Conversation 2

Curt Thank you all for join this Earthquake Workshop, Daniel and I will share some knowledge about what you should do when earthquake occurs.

感謝各位參加地震研習營，丹尼爾和我將與各位分享地震時該怎麼辦的相關知識。

Daniel First, please don't feel panic if you feel a slight shake. However, if you feel the ground began shaking violently, you should leave the building as soon as possible.[1]

首先，如果感受輕微搖晃時，請勿慌張。如果覺得地面搖晃劇烈的話，應該盡速離開這棟大樓。

Curt Before you leave, please turn off the power or unplug nearby you. [2] Do not jam together when you leave, and remember not to take the elevator. [3]

離開之前，請關掉身邊的電源或拔掉插頭。離開時請勿推擠，切記不要搭電梯。

Daniel When arrive outside, please find a clear space and do not close to any building.

順利到達公司外面時，記得找空曠的地方，請不要靠近任何建築物。

Curt If you are driving, the best way is to slow down and pull over slowly.[4]

如果剛好在開車，最好的做法是減速慢行，慢慢靠近路邊。

Daniel If you are at home, do remember shut off the gas, in case fire breaks out. [5]

如果在家，還要記得關閉瓦斯爐，以免發生火災。

Curt	Moreover, open the door, so it's easier when you escape.	還有，要把大門打開，方便逃生。
Daniel	Until now, does anyone have any question?	說到這裡，大家有沒有疑問呢？
Curt	Let's move on if there is no question.	沒有的話，我們繼續吧。
Daniel	If you cannot get to a clear space, then you can stay at the corner and cover your head with your arm.[6]	如果你無法逃到空曠的地方，只好待在牆角，用手護住頭。
Curt	If electricity is out or you cannot get through, please stay where you are and waiting for rescue.[7]	停電或手機不通的話，請待在原地等待救援。
Daniel	Usually, it followed by many aftershocks. Therefore, we should not overlook them.	通常地震後都伴隨有餘震，大家千萬不可以輕忽。
Curt	Strong aftershocks could also cause huge damages.	強烈的餘震也可能造成災害喔。
Daniel	OK, that's all for this workshop. The company prepared some earthquake kits for each Department, please come forward and gets them.	好啦，課上到此結束。公司準備有地震就難包給各部門，請大家來領取吧。

實用應答小撇步 2

① Rush out of door / Get down quickly / Stay away from windows

快點衝出門外／盡快趴下／遠離窗戶

② Please turn off the lighting / Turn on emergency lights / Please shine your flashlight

請關掉電燈／打開緊急照明／請點亮你的手電筒

③ Don't panic / Please do not push / Remember do not turn on the power right away

不要驚慌／千萬不要推擠／切記不要馬上打開電源

④ Walk down the stairs slowly / Move your feet slowly

慢慢走下樓梯／緩慢移動腳步

⑤ Switch off when leaving / Check the gas pipe / Please turn off the faucet tight

隨手關燈／檢查瓦斯管線／請關緊水龍頭

⑥ Stay side of the bed and cover your head with a pillow / Hide under the table and cover your face with your arms

躲在床旁邊，用枕頭護住頭／躲在桌子下，用手護住臉

⑦ Please do not walk around / Please calm down and call for help

請勿亂走動／請冷靜並打電話求救

💬 單字與句型

1. inflammable *adj.* 易燃的
   flam有火焰的意思，able是可能、有能力的意思。同義詞還有flammable、combustible。

2. first aid kit 醫藥箱

3. keep vigilant 保持警覺

4. disaster relief 救災、賑災

5. workshop *n.* 研習營

6. contingency plan 緊急應變計畫

7. unplug *v.* 拔掉插頭
   plug作名詞時，是插頭的意思。作動詞使用有接上插頭的意思，所以相反的，拔掉插頭就是unplug。

8. jam together 擠在一起
   People jammed together to get a good view of the famous movie star. 群眾擠在一起就為了一睹電影明星風采。

9. pull over 停車靠路邊

10. fire breaks out 發生火災

11. aftershock *n.* 餘震
    前震寫作foreshock，亦即發生在主震之前的地震。

12. overlook *v. n.* 輕忽
    The overlooked effects of global change are very dangerous. 輕忽地球變化的影響，是很危險的。

13. earthquake kit 地震救難包

14. rush out of 衝出去、衝去
    Shoppers get a rush out of bargains. 購物人潮衝向特價會。

15. faucet *n.* 水龍頭

練習題

Please complete a To Do List when meeting earthquake.

√ Turn off the _____.

√ _____.

√ _____, if you are driving.

√ Prepare _____ and _____ in normal times.

請歸類遇到地震時應該做的事情。

√ 關水龍頭

√ 拔掉插頭

√ 開車的話，停車靠路邊

√ 平時準備地震救難包與醫藥箱

解 答

1. faucet

2. Unplug

3. Pull over

4. earthquake kit

5. first aid kit

Unit 03 突然闖進公司 Strangers Break Into Company

對話 1 Conversation 1

Heather	Hi, Irene. Do you remember where we put the employee training manual?	嗨，艾琳。妳記得員工訓練手冊放到哪裡去了嗎？
Irene	Isn't it at the file cabinet?	不是就在這文件櫃子裡嗎？
Heather	Ah, yes, there it is. Thanks. But it seems a few pages are missing.	啊，找到了。謝謝。不過好像少了幾頁。
Irene	How come? Maybe you should look more carefully. ①	怎麼會呢？妳再仔細找找吧。
Heather	I still don't see it. OK, Irene, why don't we recall the contents of those missing pages.	還是沒看見。這樣吧，艾琳，我們一起回想這些缺頁的內容。
Irene	All right. Which pages are they?	好吧。到底是哪幾頁呢？
Heather	Let me see, it seems the topic of "What if you met a stranger breaks into the company suddenly?".	我看看，好像是「如果遇到陌生人突然闖進公司怎麼辦？」。
Irene	Oh, those pages. It's easy. First, ask the purpose of visit and if he	哦，這幾頁啊。那很容易呀。首先，問明來意，如

	couldn't answer that or you feel any suspicious about him, just inform the security. ②	果對方答不上來或者覺得形跡可疑，就通知大樓警衛。
Heather	And if he is carrying suspicious items, we need to evacuate staff at the office except informing security and police. ③	然後，如果他有攜帶可疑物品，除了通知警衛以及報警，還要疏散同事。
Irene	When evacuating, turn off the power and open windows.	疏散的同時要關閉電源，以及打開窗戶。
Heather	Yes, and during the time of waiting, communicate with him with patience. ④	對的。等待的同時，也要耐心地和對方溝通。
Irene	If he is here to harass any colleague, then we should call the police. Never let him get into the office. ⑤	如果他是來騷擾我們任何一位同事的話，就報警處理。千萬不能讓對方進到公司裡。
Heather	But should investigate the cause after that. If there is any colleague has been involved in an unlawful campaign, then we should let the police know. ⑥	不過事後還是要調查事件的起因。如果有同仁涉及不法，都應該通知警方。
Irene	So, I guess that's all?	我想差不多就是這些了吧。
Heather	OK, thanks for your help, Irene.	好吧，謝謝妳的幫忙，艾琳。
Irene	Sure, any time.	隨時候教。

實用應答小撇步 **1**

① Check again more carefully / Ask again more carefully

再仔細檢查／再詳細詢問

② Call the police if you feel in danger / Press the emergency button if you noticed anything wrong

覺得危險的話，就打電話報警／察覺異狀的話，就按下求救鈴

③ Except maintaining the closed circuit television regularly, and install new ones / We need to do the excise except training regularly

除了定期維修監視器設備，還要加裝新的／除了定期教育訓練，還要演練

④ To convince him(her) to calm down / To persuade him(her) to give up(surrender) / Try to be reasonable with him(her)

勸對方冷靜下來／說服對方放棄（投降）／試著和對方講道理

⑤ Keep him from the door / Must refuse letting her in

把他擋在門外／一定要拒絕讓她進門

What was the cause of this thing? / Why would (How could) this happen? / The cause of this thing is unknown (We don't know why this happen)

這件事情的起因是什麼？／怎麼會發生這件事情？／這件事的起因不明

⑥ Should inform the Executive / Should let the victim's family know / Please inform me (let me know)

應該通知公司高層／應該通知受害人家屬／請通知我

對話 2 | Conversation 2

Osmond	Hi, Richie. We have a little problem at the reception, and I need your help. ①	嗨，里奇。接待處出了點狀況，我需要你的支援。
Richie	What's going on?	什麼事？
Osmond	There is a man, scruffy and untidy, says he wants to see Michael Lin from Production Department.	有個衣衫不整的男人，說要找生產部的林麥克經理。
Richie	We don't have Michael Lin, maybe he is looking for the wrong guy. ②	我們公司沒有林麥克，他找錯人了吧。
Osmond	But he insist, what should I do?	但是他堅持有，我該怎麼辦？
Richie	Calm down. Right, did you call the security? ③	冷靜一下。對了，你打電話給大樓警衛了嗎？
Osmond	Not yet, I will call immediately.	還沒有，我馬上打。
Richie	And, does he bring any suspicious items with him? ④	還有，他有沒有攜帶可疑物品？
Osmond	Like what?	例如什麼？
Richie	I don't know, something like a package, suitcase, or anything looks dangerous? ⑤	我不曉得，就是像包裹、手提箱，或者任何看起來危險的物品？
Osmond	Well, doesn't look like he has any.	嗯，看不出來有。但是藏

	But I don't know if there is any under his coat.	在外套裡面的我就不知道了。
Richie	That sounds not so good. Does he look like a normal person? ⑥	真是糟糕。他看起來精神正常嗎？
Osmond	Except looking untidy and looking for the wrong guy? I guess yes.	除了衣衫不整、找錯人以外？我想是吧。
Richie	We should be careful about him. Did the security come yet?⑦	我們還是小心點，警衛來了嗎？
Osmond	I am busy in talking with you, haven't inform them yet.	我正忙著和你講話，還沒有通知呢。
Richie	I am on my way now, you can call them.	我這就出去，你可以打電話通知警衛了。

實用應答小撇步 2

① I need to consult with my supervisor / You need permission to get through

我需要請示主管／你需要獲得允許才能通行

② Maybe he got the wrong person / You are at the wrong building / I'm sorry, but we have no one by that name here

可能他認錯人了／你走錯大樓了／這裡沒有妳要找的人

③ Did you call 911？/ Did you press the fire alarm?

你打119了嗎？／你按下火警警報器了嗎？

④ Do you have any dangerous good in your handbag? / No inflammable items

請問你的手提袋裡有任何危險物品嗎？／這裡禁止攜帶易燃物品進入

⑤ Any object that looks suspiciously like explosives/ Any unknown liquid

任何疑似爆裂物的東西／任何不名液體

⑥ You look tired / He looks lethargic / This is freaky

你看起來有點累／他看起來精神不濟／這是瘋子的行為

⑦ Keep an eye on him / Keep my eyes open

看著他點／我會留意的

單字與句型

1. employee training manual　員工訓練手冊
2. file cabinet　文件櫃
3. suspicious *adj.*　可疑的
   也有受到懷疑的、存有懷疑的意思。

   The police are suspicious of him.　警方認為他可疑（警方正懷疑著他）。

4. evacuate *v.*　疏散、撤離
   名詞寫作evacuation。

   緊急疏散計畫為emergency evacuation plan。

5. unlawful campaign　不法的活動
6. emergency button　緊急按鈕、求救鈴
   也寫作panic button。

7. closed circuit television　監視器
   簡稱CCTV。

8. reasonable *adj.*　講道理的、有道理的
   反義詞為unreasonable。

   He is an unreasonable man.　他是個不講道理的人。

9. cause *n.*　起因、理由
   此為名詞，也可以做動詞使用，導致、使發生、引起的意思。

   What caused this fire?　是什麼導致（引起）了這場火災？

10. scruffy and untidy　邋遢的
    scruffy是邋遢的意思。untidy有蓬頭垢面與邋遢的意思。

11. explosives *n.*　爆裂物
12. lethargic *adj.*　精神不濟
    形容看起來昏昏沉沉的樣子。

💬 練習題

Please make a line match then English and Chinese.

連連看。

- closed circuit television
- suspicious
- explosives
- emergency button
- employee training manual
- file cabinet
- unlawful

- 緊急按鈕
- 不法的
- 文件櫃
- 爆裂物
- 監視器
- 可疑的
- 員工訓練手冊

💬 解 答

按照英文的順序

1. 監視器
2. 可疑的
3. 爆裂物
4. 緊急按鈕
5. 員工訓練手冊
6. 文件櫃
7. 不法的

主題 ❼ 突發狀況 Unexpected Situations

職場補給站：五個步驟搞定辦公室突發狀況

在我們教育環境中，似乎教導孩子們「循規蹈矩 (follow the rules)」的時候比應付突發狀況的時候還要多；久而久之，出了社會的職場人，對於各種職場上的突發狀況，也顯得應對笨拙。這些突發狀況除了工作上的，例如：客戶臨時改行程、改見面地點、改訂貨數量、改付款方式……等等，也包含突如其來的辦公場所的狀況，諸如：較大的地震、火警、陌生人闖入……等等。

以下就針對辦公室的突發狀況，建議行動計畫(action plans)：

❶ 鎮定、勿驚慌(calm down and don't be panic)。如果全部的人擠向同一個出口，一定造成疏散困難；所以遇到需要緊急離開的狀況時(例如：火警)，最好先鎮定下來，有秩序地往出口快速移動。如果是陌生人執意闖入，或者不合常理(unusual)的行為、動作出現，首先也是要冷靜判斷，對方只是自我無法控制的行為還是惡意的(on purpose)找碴；如果是前者，可以慢慢溝通，並且請通知大樓警衛，如果是後者，除了通知大樓警衛，還可以向地區警察報案(call the police)。

❷ 確認、確認、再確認(confirm and confirm again)。例如，剛開始輕微地震的時候，很多人會以為是自己頭暈，所以可以向身邊的人確認是不是對方也感覺到地震？火警警鈴響時，也可以向大樓管理員或警衛確認，是演習還是有火災？遇到來意不明的訪客(visitor)，也可以再三確認，對方要找的人是不是公司裡的同事或主管，就連同英文名字的人，有時候也有好多位，所以要確認對方究竟是要找哪一位同仁。

❸ 向第一線主管通報(report to first line manager)。如果遇到緊急狀況，請

向現場第一線主管通報；例如：百貨專櫃可以向所屬店長或者樓層管理主管通報，辦公室人員則可以向行政管理部門經理通報，由他們決定如何處理。

❹ 定期演習(plan exercises)。臨危可以不亂就是因為累積夠多的經驗，所以才需要演習、演練災害發生的時刻。除了大樓測試警報系統等的順暢，人員也應該參與災害發生的演習，包含逃生動線(escape routes)。

❺ 編制緊急應變小組(organize an emergency control center)。多數公司並沒有這樣的編制，特別是在公安事件(public security)發生的時候，例如：食品安全疑慮、產品導致的危險、環境汙染⋯⋯等，不但造成公司上下群龍無首，也會給外界公司治理不佳的印象。通常應變小組的負責人是公司總經理或者執行長，對外發言可能是副總或者公共關係主管(public relations manager)，如此可以統一發言，不易造成資訊的混淆；當然，這個小組對於各種公司突發狀況也需要在平時加以演練。

Part
Eight

投票表決
Let's Vote

Unit 01 有哪些投票方式
Different Ways to Vote

對話 1 Conversation 1

Len	Olivia, you're looking good! Don't look like the patient who just took sick leave.	奧莉維亞，你看起來氣色真不錯！一點也不像剛請過病假的人。
Olivia	Thanks. I still feel dizzy.	謝了。我的頭還是有點暈。
Len	So, what are you up to?	所以妳在忙什麼呢？
Olivia	Preparing for the vote of our staff trip. Didn't you hear of it? This needs to be done by tomorrow.	準備我們的員工旅遊地點投票作業啊。你沒聽說嗎？明天就要完成這項工作。
Len	How does it progress? [1] Explain me. [2]	怎麼進行呢？解釋給我聽吧。
Olivia	Fine, then everyone knows later on through the whole company. Save my time of explaining to everybody.	也好，等下全公司就都知道了。我也就省了解釋的時間。
Len	Hey, did I smell something in the air?	嘿，我是不是聞到空氣中的火藥味呀。
Olivia	All right, we should stop making jocks. First, the first round of	好了，別開玩笑了。首先，第一輪投票是各部門

218

	voting is each Department provides the top two travel destinations where they want to visit most. ③	提出他們最想要去的前兩名地點。
Len	Well, our Department has decided. They are Japan and Korea.	嗯，我們部門已經決定好了，就是日本、韓國。
Olivia	OK. Then I will announce the idea travel destinations from each Department, and putting on vote for all employees. ④	好。然後我會公布各部門的理想地點，讓全公司的職員投票。
Len	In fact, I prefer to go to other countries except these two, because I have already visited them.	其實我個人比較希望去這兩個國家以外的地點，因為我去過了。
Olivia	You see, you know what I was trying to do. Allowing other people to have more options. ⑤	你看，你知道我的用意了吧。讓其他人有機會有更多的選擇。
Len	One person, one vote? ⑥	一人一票嗎？
Olivia	Yes. The place that got the highest vote is where we will go. Moreover, it's secret ballot, so other people won't know what you vote for. ⑦	是的。最高票就是我們要去的地方囉。還有，是不記名投票，所以其他人不會知道你投了什麼。
Len	That's what I need! Olivia, you are so clever.	這正是我要的！奧莉維亞，妳真是太聰明了。
Olivia	You are welcome. Hope you got what you wished for.	哪裡。希望你如願以償喔。

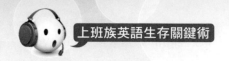
實用應答小撇步 1

① What are the rules of voting? / Please explain the ways to vote

投票規則有哪些？／請説明投票方式

② I don't (quite) follow you / He has questions about the voting rules / Could somebody explain (to) me?

我聽不懂／他對於投票規則有疑問／有誰可以解釋給我聽嗎？

③ only the top three candidates are elected / You can select your favorite top five

只有得票數最多的前三名當選／妳可以勾選最喜歡的前五項

④ citizens who over twenty years old have the right to vote / only people who have more than one year of seniority can vote / contract employees cannot vote

滿20歲以上的公民都有投票權／只有年資一年以上的人才可以投票／約聘的工讀生不能參加投票

⑤ Do I have other choices (What other options do I have)? / He seems has no other choices / Do you have Plan B?

我還有其他選擇嗎？／他似乎沒有其他的選擇了／你們有沒有備案？

⑥ One man, two votes / Multiple answers (choices) allowed / He voted an abstention

一人兩票／可以重複勾選／他投了廢票

⑦ Please write down the candidate's name you want to vote for / For this vote, please write down your name on the ballot

請在選票上寫下想要投的候選人名字／這次投票，請在選票上寫下自己的名字

對話 2 | Conversation 2

Wayne	Zoe, what's up？	佐伊，妳在忙嗎？
Zoe	Good. What?	還好。有事嗎？
Wayne	You see, it's the year-end gifts for our clients. I have been thinking is there any way makes everybody happy. ①	是這樣的，就是年終送客戶的禮品。我在想有什麼好方法可以讓大家皆大歡喜。
Zoe	What are you saying?	什麼意思？
Wayne	You know, the gift which the Executive decided to give last year, seems no client liked it.	妳知道的，就是去年公司高層決定送客戶的禮物，好像客戶們都不喜歡。
Zoe	Oh, that's really bad. So, what you going to do this year? ②	喔，這真是糟糕。所以你今年打算怎麼做呢？
Wayne	I am thinking why not let everybody vote.	我想不如讓大家投票決定吧。
Zoe	I agree with you. In this case, I should do the market research first, you know, asking clients what they want for gifts.	我支持你。這樣的話，我應該先做市場調查，你知道的，問問客戶們想要什麼禮品。
Wayne	There you go! OK, so each person provides two proposals of what to give and put on vote. The one that win the highest number of votes won.	說得好！這樣好了，每個人提出兩個禮品方案，讓大家票選。得票最高的那一個當選。

Zoe	Majority voting rules, right?	多數同意規則，對吧？
Wayne	Yes, or you can call it "the winner takes it all".	是的，你也可以說是贏家全拿。
Zoe	Will it be secret ballot? Because I think this method is more private.	是不記名投票嗎？因為我覺得這種投票方式比較有隱密性。
Wayne	You mean, if someone's proposal is eliminated...	你是說，萬一有人的提案落選的話……
Zoe	Could be bad, yes, that's what I mean.	很難看，對的，這就是我的意思。
Wayne	This is a good idea. Or one person, two votes? Or the Top Three selected so we can give one of these three gifts based on client preference. ⑥	這是個好方法。或者每個人兩票呢？又或者，得票最高的前三者當選，然後我們可以依據客戶的喜好三擇一贈送。
Zoe	I see what you mean. So, one person, two votes, and elect three of them. ⑦	我懂你的意思。那就每人兩票，最後選出三個禮品吧。

實用應答小撇步 2

① You cannot make everybody happy / The colleagues are satisfied with the vote results / The vote result makes everybody unhappy

你無法做到讓大家都滿意／同事們都很滿意這次投票結果／投票的結果讓大家很不滿意

② How did we(you) do it last year? / It's different way from this year to before / Can we do it a different way?

去年是怎麼做的呢？／今年和以往的做法不同／能不能換點不同的做法？

③ Let's vote by show of hands / What's the most Managers' options? /

大家舉手表決吧／大部分主管的意見為何？

④ These two have the same vote-getting / Here are the Top Ten selected / He fails to be elected

這兩個得票數一樣多／這裡是前10名中選的／他落選了

⑤ If hale of the people disagree / If most of the colleagues do not agree / Suppose no one wants to go to vote

如果二分之一的人不同意的話／如果大多數同事不贊同的話／假設沒有人要投票的話

⑥ decision based on Boss preference / choose Top Five according to the vote result

根據老闆的喜好決定／根據投票結果選前五名

⑦ one person, three votes, and the winner is who get the highest number of votes / the last five is eliminated

一人三票，贏家就是獲得最高票的那位／淘汰最後五名

💬 單字與句型

1. dizzy *adj.* 頭暈

2. first round of voting 第一輪投票
   第二輪投票寫作the second round of voting。

3. One person, one vote 一人一票
   也可以寫作One man, one vote。

4. secret ballot 無記名投票

5. seniority *n.* 年資

6. multiple answers (choices) 多選題、重複勾選
   free response 簡答題。

   Multiple-choice 選擇題。在英語用法上，這個詞基本上是指單選的意思；如果題目要選出一種以上的答案，通常會註明：答案為一個以上(more than one answer)；或者寫成Multiple answers (choices)。

7. abstention *n.* 廢票、棄權票
   There were two abstentions. 有兩票棄權。

   也有抑制、戒除的意思。

   abstention from drinks 戒酒。

8. ballot *n.* 選票
   此單詞與vote相同，動詞和名詞同型。

9. be eliminated 被淘汰
   名詞為elimination。其他寫法還有dumped out 、rule out；rule out在醫學上還有排除罹患某疾病的意思。

   The actress doesn't rule out such a role. 這位女演員不排斥演這個角色。

10. vote by show of hands 舉手表決

11. vote-getting 得票數
    得票率為voter turnout，voter指投票的人，turnout指聚集的人群、出席者。

💬 **練習題**

Please make a line match then English and Chinese.

連連看。

- abstention
- multiple choices
- first round of voting
- seniority
- ballot
- vote by show of hands

- 第一輪投票
- 年資
- 棄權
- 多選題
- 選票
- 舉手表決

💬 **解　答**

1. 棄權
2. 多選題
3. 第一輪投票
4. 年資
5. 選票
6. 舉手表決

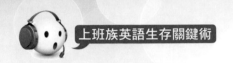

Unit 02 進行投票作業 Voting Procedures

對話 1 Conversation 1

Nita	Hi, Martina. I am here to help.

嗨,瑪堤娜。我來幫你了。

Martina	Thanks. I am beat up by the location decision voting of year-end banquet.

謝啦,這次年終尾牙的地點票選活動還真是累人。

Nita	I heard, that's why I am here. So, where do we start?

我聽說了,所以我來啦。所以,我們從哪裡開始呢?

Martina	Let's start with writing how to proceed to the vote. ①

就從寫投票作業該如何進行開始吧。

Nita	Yes, that sounds important. You can name them and I write them down.

嗯,這很重要。你說我寫吧。

Martina	OK. First, the voting day is two O'clock on December, first. At Meeting Room. ②

好的。首先,投票日在12月1日下午兩點鐘。地點在會議室。

Nita	No problem.

沒問題。

Martina	Each employee in the company can go to vote, including contracted

公司同仁,包含約聘或者工讀生,都可以參加投

	or part-time workers. After you show the employee ID card, you can get one vote. ③	票。出示員工證之後，就可以領取一張選票。
Nita	Slow down, I don't type that fast. OK, now, go on.	慢點，我打字不夠快。好了，接著説吧。
Martina	Voters should prevent the ballot from getting any ink smudges. ④ They only can click by using the pens we provided.	投票者不能在選票上做任何記號。只能使用我們提供的筆打勾。
Nita	Sounds reasonable. What else?	聽起來很合理。然後呢。
Martina	Then fold the ballot, put it in the voting box and that's all. ⑤	然後將選票摺疊起來，投進投票箱裡就可以啦。
Nita	Wait a second. Who's going to open all the ballot boxes and count all votes? ⑥	等等，誰來開票呢？
Martina	Of course the part-time workers will do.	當然是工讀生們。
Nita	What? You mean they have to pour out all the votes？ Why don't we post the locations' names on those voting boxes, and let everybody put directly inside them? ⑦	什麼？他們還要倒出來數選票？為什麼不直接在投票箱外面寫上地點的名稱，直接將選票投進去不就好了。
Martina	see what you mean. Yes, I think it's a good idea. Thanks for the suggestion, Nita.	我懂妳的意思。對，我想這是個好點子。謝謝妳的建議，妮塔。

227

實用應答小撇步 1

① The voting procedure this time is easier (more complex) than last time / Who is responsible for the voting procedure?

這次投票作業比上次簡單（複雜）／誰負責投票作業？

② The vote is beginning on the first day and ending on the fifth day in July / Please vote before one thirty on twenty-fifth

你可以在7月1日到5日之間去投票／請在25日下午一點半以前完成投票

③ After you reply, the system will send the vote to your E-Mail address / After input ID and cell phone number, then you can vote

回信後，系統會自動寄送選票到你的電子郵箱／輸入身分證字號與手機號碼後，就可以投票了

④ Keep ballots clean / Cannot sign on the ballot / Cannot tear up a voting ballot

保持選票乾淨／不能在選票上簽名／不能撕毀選票

⑤ Place the ballot face down / Put the ballot into an envelope

將選票正面朝下／將選票放進信封裡

⑥ There will be five colleagues responsible for counting the votes / The result of vote will be announced on the next day

會有五個同仁負責開票作業／開票結果會在隔天公佈

⑦ Send directly by E-Mail / Deliver the circled results to Manager directly

直接以電子郵件寄出／直接將圈選的結果交給主管

對話 **2** Conversation **2**

Mitchell	Samuel, did you get the notice? ①	你收到通知了嗎？
Samuel	Yes. Our Manager asked me to work with you on designing voting procedures.	有啊。我們經理要我和你一起設計線上投票作業。
Mitchell	That's right. Should we start now?	對。我們現在開始？
Samuel	Sure. What's on your mind?	好啊。你有什麼想法？
Mitchell	First, voting period is five days. ② Voting hours are 9 AM to 5 PM.	首先，投票期間為五天。投票時間是早上9點到下午5點。
Samuel	Got you.	沒問題。
Mitchell	Each person has one vote, and it is an abstention if you don't vote before the time expires. ③	一人一次投票機會，如果過期沒有投就是棄權。
Samuel	OK, they are easy to set. So, log in by what identity? ④	好的，這很容易設定。用什麼證明登入投票呢？
Mitchell	Employee ID number. Wait, plus personal ID number for two-factor authentication.	員工證號碼。等等，要加上身份證字號的雙重認證。
Samuel	Do you want to see who vote for what from backend? ⑤	你要設定後台可以看見誰投了什麼嗎？
Mitchell	For the privacy, I don't think so.	為了隱私，我想不要好了。

Samuel	OK, you are the boss.	好的，你説了算。
Mitchell	Statistical results can also be set from here? ⑥	統計結果也可以從這邊設定嗎？
Samuel	Yes, they can. Do you need any specific setting?	沒問題啊，需要什麼特別的設定嗎？
Mitchell	I would like to classify the data by department, gender and age. It would be perfect, if it can analysis right after finishing vote count and send to me. ⑦	我想要依照部門別、性別和年齡做分析。⑦ 如果可以在投票後馬上做統計，然後寄給我，是最好的。
Samuel	OK, let me see what I can do for you.	好的，我來看看怎麼幫你吧。

實用應答小撇步 2

① Just to inform you that / Just to let you know that / Please be informed that

只是要通知你／只是要讓你知道／請知悉以下事項

② The date of voting (polling date) is from second to eighth / Voting period is non-holiday (non-office hour)

投票日從2號到8號／投票期間為非假日（非辦公時間）

③ an abstention is not a vote / Please do not vote an abstention

棄權就不算有投票／請勿投廢票或棄權

④ What ID do I need to show to vote? / Please bring identification with photo to vote

投票時需要出示什麼證明？／請攜帶有照片的證件前往投票

⑤ David voted YES (NO) / Nine votes cast, five yes, three no, one abstention / No one saw him coming to vote

大衛投了贊成票（反對票）／有九個人投票，五個人投贊成票、三個人投反對票 ，一個棄權／沒有人看見他來投票

⑥ Please E-Mail General Manager the statistical results / It seems that there is a problem with the statistical results / Please set the system and allow the statistical results to be sent directly after finishing vote count

請E-Mail給總經理投票的統計結果／投票的統計結果似乎有問題／請設定統計結果在開票結束後自動寄出

⑦ Analysis by where branches locate / Analysis by different date of voting

依照分公司所在地進行統計分析／依照不同投票日期做分析

單字與句型

1. I am beat up.　我累壞了
   關於累的口語還有：
   I am burnt out from my job.　我被工作折磨得好累。（強調心理上的累）
   I am exhausted (tired) from studying all night.　我熬夜讀書，實在好累呀。

2. year-end banquet　年終尾牙
   banquet是宴會、宴請的意思。

3. ink smudge　印記

4. voting box　投票箱

5. count the votes　數選票、開票
   也可以寫成vote count。

6. circled *adj.*　圈選的
   circled by red　以紅色圈選的。

7. voting period　投票期間

8. voting hour *v.*　投票時間

9. expire *v.*　到期、期滿
   My lease will expire on October 30th of this year.　我的租約到今年10月30日到期。

10. two-factor authentication　雙重認證
    亦即需要兩道手續，來確認該使用者就是本人。例如，賓士車的晶片車鑰匙(car key with chip)+指紋(fingerprint)，就運用雙重認證的概念。

11. statistical results　統計的結果

12. classify *v.*　分類
    名詞為classification。

💬 練習題

- Please _____.
- Who will responsible for _____?
- The _____ is company's _____.
- Please put _____ at the Meeting Room.
- Company's lease will _____ on January 30th of next year.

- 請將統計結果分類。
- 誰負責開票呢？
- 投票期間剛好是公司年終尾牙。
- 請將投票箱放到會議室。
- 辦公室租約在明年一月三十日到期。

💬 解 答

1. Classify
2. statistical results
3. counting the votes
4. voting period
5. year-end banquet
6. voting boxes
7. expire

Unit 03 公佈結果 Announce the Results

Angelica	Hi, Hector. Did you finish counting the votes? [1]	嗨,海克特。你統計完這次票選結果了嗎?
Hector	Not yet. It's a little complex.	還沒。有點複雜呢。
Angelica	What's the story?	怎麼說?
Hector	I think it's because we didn't plan it well, now somebody used a pencil. And look at this all kinds of colors, I can barely read these votes. [2]	我想是因為一開始沒有規劃好,有人用鉛筆。還有看看這各種顏色,我根本無法閱讀這些選票。
Angelica	Poor you. Is there anything I can help?	好可憐喔。有什麼我可以幫忙的嗎?
Hector	Great! Why don't you responsible for recognizing the unknown votes? [3]	太好了!妳負責辨識不清楚的選票吧。
Angelica	OK. Let me see them. Well, it seems that there are twelve of them cannot be recognized. [4]	好吧。讓我看看。嗯,好像有十二張無法辨識。
Hector	Then they are abstentions.	那麼就只能算是廢票了。
Angelica	What a shame. And here are three	真可惜。還有這三張圈選

	votes all have two items circled.	了兩個以上的選項耶。
Hector	They are abstentions, too. All right, so here are total one hundred and twenty two votes, minus fifteen abstentions.	也是廢票。好了，總共是一百二十二張，扣掉十五張廢票。
Angelica	How many people voted YES? I am so nervous about the announcement of the results.	有多少人投贊成票？結果要公布了，我好緊張喔。
Hector	Seventy six, means there is a seventy one percentage of people voted YES.	七十六張，等於是百分之七十一的人贊成。
Angelica	Wow, that's great. I bet Alice that it must be more people voted YES.	哇，太好了。我和愛麗絲打賭一定是贊成的人比較多。
Hector	Congratulation, you've won. ⑦	恭喜妳贏了。
Angelica	Thank you. See you later.	謝謝你，待會兒見？
Hector	Thanks for the help. See you later.	謝謝妳的幫忙。待會兒見。

實用應答小撇步　1

① When vote count can be done? / Please finish vote count before knocking off time

什麼時候可以統計完成？／請在下班前統計完成

② It's hard to read these votes / I cannot read (recognize, identify) this vote / These votes are all dirty

這些選票很難閱讀／我無法辨識這張選票／這些選票都髒了

③ He is responsible for counting YES(NO) votes (abstention) / Could you please supervise the procedure of opening all the ballot boxes and count all votes

他負責數贊成票（反對票）／可以請妳負責監督開票過程嗎？

④ There are seven votes broken / Some people didn't go to vote / What to do with the unknown votes

有七張選票破了／有些人沒有投票／無法辨識的選票怎麼辦？

⑤ How many people did not vote? / Who didn't vote? / Did everybody vote?

有多少人沒有去投票？／誰沒有投呢？／大家都投了嗎？

⑥ Those voting NO are in the majority / There is a ten percentage abstention / The number of people who voted for YES reached a historical high

反對票佔大多數／有一成的比例是廢票／贊成的人達到歷史新高

⑦ The winner is David / I am happy for you that you won / It's a shame that he lost

贏家是大衛／妳贏了，我真替妳高興／很可惜他輸了

對話 2 Conversation 2

Cliff	Rita, are you in the middle of something? [1]	莉塔，妳正在忙著嗎？
Rita	Don't you see? I am counting the votes.	你沒有看到嗎？我正在計算選票啊。
Cliff	Oh, now I see it. So, do you need a hand? [2]	哦，看見了。怎麼樣，要不要幫忙？
Rita	That would be wonderful. Look carefully, each one means a YES vote. Now we are counting how many one that each new product got.	再好不過了。注意看著，1代表投贊成票。現在我們要看每個新產品一共有幾個 1。
Cliff	It's not so difficult, but since there were too many people vote, so needs patience to calculate them.	不是很難，但是因為投票人很多，所以要耐心統計。
Rita	I knew that you are suitable for this job. I am giddy already.	我就知道這工作適合你來。我已經看得眼都花了。
Cliff	Can we start counting from fewer votes?[3] It seems that cartoon characters are less welcomed, only got five votes. [4]	不如先從得票數少的開始統計？我看卡通人物的好像不受歡迎，只有五票。
Rita	Yes. The Sakura flower one seems won fewer votes, too. [5] Let	嗯。櫻花圖案的好像得票數也很少，我看看，一共

	me check, it's eighteen totally.	是十八票。
Cliff	Graffiti seems got more votes than the other two.⑥ Thirty four totally. Did you get them down?	街頭塗鴉的好像比前面兩個獲得的票數都多。一共是三十四票。妳都登記下來了？
Rita	Oh, real bad! Could you repeat them again?	喔，糟糕！你可以重複一下嗎？
Cliff	My God, Rita, could you focus on, please? They are five, eighteen, and thirty four.	我的天，莉塔，專心一點好嗎？五、十八、三十四。
Rita	Done. I got them all wrote down.	沒問題，都記下來了。
Cliff	The last one is national flags, surprised won the most of votes. ⑦	最後剩下世界國旗的圖案，意外地贏得了大多數的選票。
Rita	What? Didn't you vote this one?	怎麼了，難道你不是投這個？
Cliff	Come on, Rita. I will not tell you the answer.	少來了，莉塔。我才不會告訴妳呢。
Rita	I get it, it's personal thing. Anyway, thank you for your help. Let's go, let me buy you a lunch.	我懂，這是個人隱私。總之，謝謝你的幫忙喔。走吧，我請你吃午餐。

實用應答小撇步 2

① Are you busy? / What are you up to? / How are you doing?

你忙嗎？／在忙些什麼呢？／你過得怎麼樣？

② You could ask him to help you / Could you do me a favor? / My hands are full, so I have no time for you

你可以請他幫忙／幫我一個忙好嗎？／我很忙，沒有空幫你

③ Start count the votes from Number One candidate / Start calculating from the left vote box / Start count the votes from this project

先從一號候選人開始統計票數／先從左邊的投票箱開始統計／從這個專案的得票數開始統計

④ He is the man of the moment at the office / He is the office nuisance

他是辦公室的風雲人物／他是辦公室的討厭鬼

⑤ This item's voter turnout was not very high / Very close vote / There is a huge vote differences between these two

這個項目的得票率不高／票數很接近／兩者票數落差太大

⑥ Got the highest votes among the three / The votes head for record low / The ballots of the winner are exactly the sum of the other two

獲得的票數是三個裡面最高的／獲得前所未見的低票數／勝出的得票數剛好是另外兩者的總和

⑦ Winning (Victory) is a par for the course / I am surprised why this item didn't win the selection

勝選是意料中事／我很意外這個項目怎麼沒有中選

單字與句型

1. knocking off time   下班時間
   也可以寫作Time to knock off，下班時間到了。

2. calculate *v.*   計算
   也有盤算、演算的意思。名詞是calculation，除了有意算的意思之外，同時也是計算機的英文。

   Calculating your monthly expenses is an important part of your daily life.   日常生活中的一個重要部分就是計算每月的生活開銷。

3. giddy *adj.*   頭暈眼花

4. less welcomed   較不受歡迎的

5. graffiti *n.*   街頭的塗鴉

6. the man of the moment   風雲人物

7. nuisance *n.*   討厭鬼

8. voter turnout   得票率

   turnover   有週轉率的意思。

   Table turnover rate   餐廳翻桌率

   Labor turnover   員工流動率

9. sum *n.*   總和
   也有概括的意思。

   I asked the accountant to sum up the bills.   我讓會計去算了一下帳單的總數。

   To sum up, education is everything.   總括來説，教育就是一切。

10. a par for the course   意料中事
    par是正常、標準桿的意思；course則是路徑。在一句話裡就是指正常的路徑、意料中的事情。

💬 練習題

- Please _____ _____.
- The _____ on the wall makes me _____.
- David is _____ at the office and it is _____.

- 請<u>計算</u>一下<u>得票率</u>。
- <u>牆上</u>的<u>街頭塗鴉</u>令我<u>頭暈眼花</u>。
- 大衛在辦公室<u>不受歡迎</u>是<u>意料中的事</u>。

💬 解　答

1. calculate
2. voter turnout
3. graffiti
4. giddy
5. less welcomed
6. a par for the course

主題 ❽ 投票表決 Let's Vote

職場補給站：辦公室裡的民主活動

投票(vote)，是民主社會最神聖的活動之一；一人一票 (one man, one vote)，用選票決定國家大事，是民主的最高象徵。

在辦公室裡面也有大小的票選活動會進行，從年度員工旅遊地點、行程、尾牙地點、菜色、表演藝人、年節禮贈品……等等；每每到了投票時刻，總是各部門同仁資訊、情感交流的時刻，大家交換著意見、分析著各項選項的優劣(pros and cons)，好不熱鬧。

不過如同現實社會裡票選活動一樣，辦公室裡的民主活動，有時候也會成為勾心鬥角的另類場合，職場人不可不小心謹慎。

以下就提供策劃辦公室票選活動的要領：

❶ 規劃流程(rundown)。諸如開始期間、截止時間、地點、動線、如何投票……等等。如果想要越少的失誤，建議寫下來後(write it down)，讓其他同事試著進行投票，從中發現可能的問題，並且盡早修改。

❷ 如果是記名投票的話，要小心資料不外流(do not disclose)。因為投票的結果總是幾家歡樂幾家愁，所以為了避免紛爭，如果是記名投票，統計時就要小心不要將「誰投了什麼」的資訊外流。

❸ 盡量少用舉手投票(vote by show of hands)。有時候對選項的表態是一件很尷尬的事情，所以不建議用公開的方式進行表決；如果用了，有些時候也會獲得「不是真心(not from a real true heart)」的統計結果。這種投票方式或稱為「面子投票」，亦即是為了保全自己的面子，或預測大多數人

可能投的選項而跟從的投票。

❹ 做好統計工作(statistic work)。有時候統計結果會用圖表或者說明，呈現給相關的主管，這個時候就要做好統計的工作。如果要表示和百分比相關的，可以使用圓餅圖(pie chart)，如果是呈現對比，可以用柱狀圖(histogram)。同樣的，為了避免收到的人看不懂，完成後最好也請同事們試著閱讀並分享看到的說明是否有誤。

Part
Nine

會議紀錄
Meeting Minutes

Unit 01 如何記錄要點 How to Take Meeting Minutes

對話 1 Conversation 1

Isaac Dine, what's the matter? You look ghastly, are you OK? [1]

黛安，怎麼了？你的臉色很難看耶，還好吧？。

Diane Oh, that is the damn meeting minutes. I don't even know where to start? [2]

喔，就是那該死的會議紀錄。我都不曉得從何下筆。

Isaac Let me see what I can do for you.

讓我看看有什麼可以幫得上忙的。

Diane You are such a nice person, Isaac.

你真好，艾薩克。

Isaac Hey, there's no such thing as a free lunch. So, it's your treat.

嘿，天下沒有白吃的午餐，所以你要請客。

Diane No problem. Look, this is my draft. [3]

沒問題。你看，這是我的初稿。

Isaac Wow, what a mess. You should write it in an order of date, time, place, present and discussion.

哇，好凌亂啊。你應該按照日期、時間、地點、出席者、討論主題的順序寫才對。

Diane It that so? No one ever taught me. [4]

是這樣嗎？從來沒有人教過我。

Isaac	Now you know that. Followed by announcements and resolution.	現在妳知道啦。然後接著是報告事項以及決議事項。
Diane	Are announcements under discussion?	討論主題下方就是報告事項嗎？
Isaac	Yes, discussion means what does the person in charge reports on a certain topic. ⑤	是呀，報告事項是指針對某個討論主題，負責人的報告有哪些。
Diane	Resolution is the decision that everybody made?	決議事項就是大家一致的決定嗎？
Isaac	That's right. And if there is anybody has objections, make sure you keep those minutes.	對呀。如果有人有反對意見，要特別記錄下來。
Diane	OK, I got that.	好，我知道了。
Isaac	You see, it's not difficult at all.	妳看，一點兒也不難。
Diane	Thanks, I owe you one. ⑦	謝了。我欠你一次。

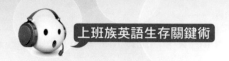

實用應答小撇步 1

① He looks washed out after his illness / My Boss always keeps his straight face / Don't pull such a long face

他生病後臉色一直很難看／老闆總是板著臉／別老是苦著臉（愁眉苦臉）

② I don't know what to say / This proposal is hard to write well / I don't know what you mean

我不曉得從何說起（我不曉得該說些什麼）／這個提案很難寫得好／我不曉得你的意思

③ This is revised / This is the final version

這是修改版／這已經是最終版了

④ No one said anything like that / I never heard of this thing / I never knew this thing

從沒有人這樣說過／我從來沒有聽說這件事／我一直都不知道這件事

⑤ What did he report during the meeting? / Your reporting during the meeting was good

他剛才在會議上都報告了哪些內容？／你在會議上的報告真棒

⑥ If there is any absence / If there is anyone has extempore motion

如果有人缺席／假設有人有臨時動議

⑦ I owe you a dinner (lunch / meal) / Do I owe you anything? / You owe me that

我欠你一頓晚餐（午餐／一頓飯）／我有（虧）欠你什麼嗎？／你欠我的

對話 **2** Conversation **2**

Greg	Bonny, I just finish my meeting minutes. Maybe you have some time to check for me?	波妮，我的會議紀錄寫好了。或許妳有空幫我確認一下？
Bonny	Could you ask Kelly to do that for you? ① I am busy right now.	可以請凱莉看嗎？我正在忙耶。
Greg	Maybe it's not a good time? ② Because Kelly said she wasn't able to attend the meeting, so you are the only one who can help.	或許我來得不是時候？凱莉已經說了她那天沒有出席會議，所以只有妳能幫忙囉。
Bonny	All right, consider it as the gift you're your last treat.	好吧，就當我還給你上次你請客的謝禮。
Greg	No problem at all! We are even. ③	沒問題！我們倆不相欠了。
Bonny	First, you forgot to put the minutes from our last meeting. ④ You know, they confirmed the progress of previous meeting minutes	首先，你忘記把之前會議紀錄的內容放進來了。你知道的，會議上一定會針對之前的進度做確認。
Greg	Indeed, I forgot to put them in.	的確，是我忘了放進來。
Bonny	There you go. Moreover, you forgot to list the actions by whom. ⑤	這就對啦。還有，你忘記列出誰要負責哪件事情。
Greg	Let me see it. I really did, didn't I . That's really bad.	我看看。還真的忘記了。真是糟糕。

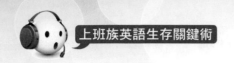

Bonny	Over all, it looks OK. But you wrote too much, this is writing an article. All you to do is to use bullet points. ⑥	整體而言，還可以。但是你寫得太多了，這不是寫一篇文章。你只要點列式紀錄就可以了。
Greg	Do you mean list them by point.	你是說一點一點的紀錄。
Bonny	Yes, don't write like making a speech or talk. The important thing is letting the readers see the important points of the meeting. ⑦	對呀，不要寫得像演講或說話一樣。重要的是讓閱讀者看見會議的重點。
Greg	I see. I will try my best to adjust them.	我懂了。我盡量調整。
Bonny	When should you hand it out?	什麼時候要交呢？
Greg	3 PM this afternoon.	今天下午三點鐘。
Bonny	Hope you make it, Greg. It's one thirty now.	希望來得及喔，格雷格。現在已經下午一點半了。

實用應答小撇步 **2**

① Take a look (Have a look) at these legal terms / Please let David look over those documents / Just a glance

看一看這些法律條款／請大衛過目這些文件／稍微看一下就好

② Not a good time? / When will it be convenient for you to check that for me?

我來得不是時候嗎？／什麼時候你才方便替我檢查？

③ I thought we were even / We've squared up with the shopkeeper

我以為我們已經互不相欠了／我們和店家的帳已經結清（兩不相欠）了

④ You forgot to write down the date of next meeting / You forgot to fill in the meeting end time

你忘記寫上下次開會日期／你忘記填上會議結束時間

⑤ Please list each project manager's name / General Manager need to know who is in charge of this project? / Who's responsible for client A now?

請列出各項專案的負責人清單／總經理需要知道這項事項的負責人是誰？／現在是誰在負責A客戶？

⑥ Just take down important points / Write down opinions from everybody clearly

只要記下重點即可／要清楚記下所有人的意見

⑦ The important thing is the contents of resolutions / The important thing is who was absent on that day

重要的是決議事項的內容／重要的是當天缺席的人有誰

🗨 單字與句型

1. meeting minutes　會議記錄
   minute除了有分鐘的意思以外，還有備忘錄、會議紀錄的意思。需要留意的是，minutes為複數。

2. ghastly *adj.*　臉色慘白的
   也有陰森的意思。

3. your treat　你請客
   我請客則是my treat。

4. discussion *n.*　討論主題
   也可以寫成topic。

5. resolution *n.*　決議事項

6. straight face　嚴肅的表情

7. keep minutes　做會議記錄
   還可以寫成take minutes。

8. revised *adj.*　修訂的
   Here is the revised edition of his proposal.　這是他提案的修正版本。

9. absence *n.*　缺席

10. extempore motion　臨時動議

11. bullet point　點列式要點
    bullet的意思是子彈，和point要點結合的話，就是點列式（列出重點）的意思。

12. square up　結清、使…一致

13. date of next meeting　下次開會日期

14. project manager　專案經理

練習題

A: I would like to see the _____ that last time took.

B: Right here.

A: I remember that there were three _____, but here are two.

B: I guess the minutes taker missed that.

A: It seems like _____ is also missed. Who took this meeting minutes?

B: It was Ginny's turn.

A: Just provide me the _____ version of it as soon as possible.

A：我想看上一次的會議紀錄。

B：就在這裡。

A：我記得決議事項有三點，但是怎麼只記錄了兩點。

B：我猜是做會議紀錄的人漏了。

A：臨時動議好像也漏了。到底是誰做的會議紀錄？

B：輪到金妮。

A：請盡快給我修訂版本吧。

解 答

1. meeting minutes

2. resolutions

3. extempore motion

4. revised

Unit 02　確認紀錄正確性　Confirm the Correctness

對話 1　Conversation 1

Laura	Albert, do you have a minute right now?	亞伯特，現在有空嗎？
Albert	Hi, Laura. I do. Why?	嗨，蘿拉。有的。怎麼了嗎？
Laura	It seems there are some problems of the draft minutes from yesterday's meeting. ①	昨天的會議紀錄的初稿有點問題。
Albert	Where are them?	哪裡有問題呢？
Laura	The first resolution, I don't remember members reached an agreement. ②	你看第一項決議，我不記得出席者達成了共識。
Albert	Let me see my note. Oh, I am really sorry. I wrote the resolution of second topic to the first one.③	我看一下我的筆記。喔，真是抱歉。我把第二項的決議寫到第一項去了。
Laura	And the last topic, I remember it was rejected by everyone. ④	還有最後一個事項，我記得大家都否決掉了。
Albert	It's really bad, isn't it? I hope you won't tell my supervisor that my	真是糟糕，希望你不會告訴主管我的會議紀錄做得

	minutes taking are down poorly.	真差勁。
Laura	You have much to learn. [5]	你還有很多要學的呢。
Albert	Thank you. So, is there anything else needs to be modified? [6]	謝謝妳。還有其他地方需要修改的嗎？
Laura	Well, that about sums it up. You can E-Mail to all attendees.	大致上是這樣吧。應該可以E-Mail給所有出席者了。
Albert	Including the absent?	缺席的人也要嗎？
Laura	Of course. Especially the General Manager, he didn't attend because he was in business trip to Europe.	當然囉。尤其是總經理，他沒出席是因為去歐洲出差了。
Albert	OK, I got you. Hey, let me buy you a drink after work? [7]	好的，我知道了。嘿，下班後我請你喝一杯吧？
Laura	No, maybe next time. I am going out with my classmate at university tonight.	不了，下次吧。今天我和大學同學約好了呢。
Albert	OK, next time.	説好了下次喔。

實用應答小撇步 **1**

① I am in doubt about the correctness of your meeting minutes / He didn't say that in the meeting / This meeting minutes is with high correctness

我對你的會議紀錄的正確性存疑／他在會議中不是這樣講的／這份會議紀錄的正確性很高

② They didn't reach a consensus on Project A in the meeting/ We reached an agreement on Topic B

會議中大家對A專案沒有共識／會議中我們達成了對B討論事項的共識

③ These two resolutions should be swapped / The order of these two topics should be swapped / We should swap their order of making a speak

這兩項的決議應該對調／這兩項的討論主題順序應該對調／我們應該對調他們兩個的發言順序

④ The General Manager ruled against the proposal / The motion is lost

提案被總經理否決了／臨時動議被否決了

⑤ I have a lot to learn from you / There is not much you can learn from him / All my knowledge is from her

我還有很多要向您學習的 / 他身上沒有什麼可以學的 / 我會的都是她教我的

⑥ It would require a drastic revision of this document / You could just modify it a little bit / Do not change even one word

這份文件需要大幅度修改／你只要稍微修改一下就行了／連一個字都不要修改

⑦ Let me take you out this evening / The drink is on me

晚上我請你去吃飯／我請喝酒（酒錢算我的）

對話 2 Conversation 2

Vanessa	Jed, may I ask you if you still remember the discussion from yesterday's meeting? ①	杰德,我想問你還記不記得昨天的會議內容?
Jed	Well, are you testing me? ②	嗯,妳是想要考考我嗎?
Vanessa	No. I think I got confused by some discussions. ③	不是啦。我想我被某些討論內容搞混了。
Jed	I see. OK, I will try my best to help. ④	這樣啊,我盡可能幫妳吧。
Vanessa	Great. I will buy you a sandwich for you.	太好了,我請你吃三明治。
Jed	Just buy me a cup of coffee. OK, what's your question?	請我喝咖啡吧。說吧,哪裡有問題?
Vanessa	Do you remember the votes of Topic A?	你記得A討論主題的票數嗎?
Jed	The resolution was approved seven to two. ⑤	七票對兩票,通過。
Vanessa	What about the extempore motion?	臨時動議呢?
Jed	Project A was approved, but not Project B. ⑥	專案A通過了,專案B沒有。
Vanessa	Which Department provided paper report yesterday?	昨天是哪一個部門提供書面報告的?

Jed	The Financial Department.	財務部門。
Vanessa	Oh, I thought it was the Sales Department.	喔，我記成是業務部了。
Jed	Anything else?	還有其他的嗎？
Vanessa	I don't think so.	沒有了。
Jed	After you finish it, you could E-Mail me and see if it needs any adjustment. ⑦	妳寫好後可以E-Mail給我，看看還有沒有要修改的地方。

實用應答小撇步 **2**

① There are few parts which I don't remember clearly / I know it by heart / Nobody expects you remember it

有幾個地方我記得不是很清楚／我可是牢記在心／沒有人期待妳會記得

② Don't test me, because I have bad memory / Her memory ability can meet any challenge

別考我，我記憶很差／她的記憶力經得起考驗

③ I am confused by the results of votes / She confused with Chairman and master of ceremonies

我被投票結果搞混了／她將會議主席和司儀搞混了

④ Please help me as could as possible / She already done what she could to help you / He didn't do his best

請盡可能幫我／她已經進一切可能來幫妳了／他沒有盡力

⑤ After discussion, members agreed / The motion is carried by thirty votes to fifteen

討論後，全體一致同意通過／臨時動議以30票對15票通過了

⑥ Only one of these two projects was approved / None of these proposals are getting approved / Yesterday's proposal were all approved

這兩個專案只有通過一個／這些提案都沒有通過／昨天的提案都通過了

⑦ To see if there is any discrepancy / To see if there is any place doesn't comform

看看有沒有出入／看看有沒有不符合的地方

💬 單字與句型

1. reach an agreement　達成共識
   也可以寫成reach a consensus。

2. reject *v.*　否決
   也可以寫成rule against。

3. that about sum it up　大致如此
   這是一句片語。

   You want me to buy milk for you, do laundry and clean the basement. Does that about sum it up?　你要我替你買牛奶、洗衣服和除草。是不是大致如此？

4. I am in doubt about...　我對⋯存疑
   也可以寫成I have a doubt about...。如果不只一項的懷疑點，a doubt可以改成複數doubts。

5. correctness *n.*　正確性
   correct為形容詞。

6. swap *v.*　對調、交換
   Do you want to swap your book with me?　你想要和我交換書籍嗎？

7. a drastic revision　大幅度的修改

8. master of ceremonies　司儀

9. discrepancy *n.*　出入、差異、差距

10. comform *v.*　相符
    也有遵守、遵照、適應的意思。

    If you don't conform to the traffic laws, you might get fined.　如果不遵守交通法規，就可能會被罰款。

練習題

- There was a _____ in the two reports of the accident.
- Most people willingly _____ to the customs of society.
- Our plan needs _____.
- Because of their intransigent attitude we were unable to _____.
- I _____ the _____ of this paper.

- 這兩則意外的報導有很大的<u>出入</u>。
- 大多數人都願意<u>遵守</u>社會習俗。
- 我們的計畫需要<u>大幅度的修改</u>。
- 因為他們強硬的態度，所以無法<u>達成共識</u>。
- 我對這篇論文的<u>正確性存疑</u>。

解　答

1. discrepancy
2. conform
3. a drastic revision
4. reach an agreement / reach a consensus
5. am in doubt about / have a doubt about
6. correctness

Unit 03 修改與發佈 Modify and Release

對話 1 Conversation 1

Phoebe	Sandy, could you E-Mail me the meeting minutes from last time?①	珊蒂，可以麻煩妳寄給我上次的會議紀錄嗎？
Sandy	You can try to look for Trash or Spam in your E-Mail box.	妳可以試著找找郵件裡的垃圾桶或垃圾郵件。
Phoebe	Actually, I deleted it accidentally. ②	其實是我不小心刪除了。
Sandy	OK. What you need it for?	好吧。妳需要它做什麼？
Phoebe	Just for reference. This time is my term of taking minutes.	只是做參考。這次輪到我寫會議紀錄。
Sandy	Oh, right. Then good luck.	喔，對喔。那祝妳好運。
Phoebe	But I have a question. How do you label it if there is a new progress on last time's minutes?	但是我有個疑問。如果上次會議紀錄有新進度的話，怎麼標註呢？
Sandy	You just use strikethrough font in red on the original minutes. ③ But the new progress part should be marked in blue. ④	在原會議紀錄上使用紅色刪除線就可以啦。但是新進度要用藍色的字表示。
Phoebe	I see.	原來如此。

Sandy	Moreover, please send it by using blind carbon copy. ⑤	還有，請用密件功能發佈。
Phoebe	Why?	為什麼？
Sandy	Normally, you don't have to. But since the representatives from our client also attended the meeting, so it is more appropriate to do so.	通常是不用這樣做，但是因為這次會議有客戶代表來參加會議。所以這樣比較妥當。
Phoebe	OK, I will remember that.	好的，我會記下來。
Sandy	When you finish it, send to Manager and let him have a look first. ⑥	寫好了可以寄給經理，請他先過目。
Phoebe	No problem. Thanks, you are so sweet.	沒問題。謝了。妳真是太貼心了。
Sandy	All right, all right. You are too mushy.	好啦好啦，少肉麻了。

實用應答小撇步 **1**

① Could you borrow me the meeting minutes from last time? / I need the meeting minutes from last time / Where are the previous meeting minutes?

麻煩你借我看上次的會議紀錄／我需要找上次的會議紀錄／上次的會議紀錄放到哪裡去了？

② I didn't mean it / This was just the result of a moment's inattention

我不是故意的／這件事只是一時不小心的結果

③ Please mark the results of votes with underline / Select the modification and highlight it by using Highlight on word

請在投票結果上用下底線標註／修改的部分用word上螢光色凸顯

④ Highlight the new progress in bold / The important discussions should be marked in red

新進度用粗體字表示／重要的討論事項應該用紅字標明

⑤ Please release to all employees / Only send to Department Manager

請發佈給公司全體員工／只要寄給各部門主管就好

⑥ For his eyes only / She has a photographic memory for detail

只能給他過目／她有過目不忘的驚人記憶力

對話 2 Conversation 2

Mimi	Hi, Johnny, excuse me for a second.	強尼，打擾一下。
Johnny	Hi, our great beauty Mimi. What I can do for you?	嗨，是大美女美美。有什麼我可以幫妳的？
Mimi	Here is the thing, I almost finish the meeting minutes from yesterday.[①] However, I am not so sure about some places, and I am thinking maybe you can check them for me?[②③]	是這樣的，昨天的會議記錄我快寫完了。但是有幾個地方不太確定，可以請你幫我看一下？
Johnny	No problem. Let me see it, well, you omitted this conclusion here.[④]	沒問題。我看看，這個結論妳漏寫了。
Mimi	Oh, right. Thanks.	喔，的確。謝謝你。
Johnny	Do remember put an underscore in a sentence when you want to use a letter to stand out.[⑤]	記得要凸顯的字句要用下底線標明。
Mimi	But I usually use boldface, it can be seen clearer.	我習慣用粗體字，這樣看得比較清楚。
Johnny	That would be fine, too.	也可以。
Mimi	Anything else?	還有其他地方嗎？

Johnny	Right, from now on, the meeting minutes should be posted on bulletin board, too. [6]	對了，從現在起，會議紀錄也要貼在公佈欄上。
Mimi	Is there no need to send E-Mails?	不用發送電子郵件了嗎？
Johnny	I mean except sending E-Mails.	我是說除了發送電子郵件以外。
Mimi	Sure, you got it.	當然，沒問題。

實用應答小撇步 2

① I am almost done in preparation for new product launch proposal next week / Project A approaches its conclusion

下週的新產品上市簡報我快準備好了／A專案已接近尾聲

② I got to make sure my career is going somewhere / Please make sure you bring everything you need for tomoroow

我必須確定我的事業有所發展／請確定明天需要的東西都帶齊了

③ You could ask your manager to check that for you / This will be needed to ask General Manager / I am not available to check that for you right now

可以請你的主管幫妳確認一下／這件事可能要去請示總經理才行／我現在沒有空幫你看

④ Here he wrote few wrong words / There is one fewer on attendance

這裡他寫錯幾個字了／出席人數少寫了一個人

⑤ Please use the track changes feature / He added few comment to the document for our reference

請用追蹤修訂功能／他在文件上添加了一些意見供我們參考

⑥ Meeting minutes should be printed out and archived / Please archive this file

會議記錄要列印一份存檔／請將這份檔案歸檔

單字與句型

1. Spam *n.* 垃圾郵件信箱
   Spam Mail就是所謂的垃圾郵件。

2. accidentally *adv.* 意外地、偶然地
   名詞是accident，意外、事故的意思。

3. label *v.* 標註
   此為作動詞使用，同義詞還有mark。label作名詞使用是標籤的意思。

4. strikethrough 刪除線
   single line strikethrough 是單線刪除線；double line strikethrough，則
   是雙刪除線的意思。

5. blind carbon copy 密件副本
   簡稱B.C.C.。副本是carbon copy，簡稱C.C.。

6. normally *adv.* 通常地、按常理說地

7. appropriate *adj.* 適當的

8. mushy *adj.* 肉麻的
   也有糊狀的、感傷的意思。

9. inattention *n.* 不注意、不小心
   attention是注意的意思，反義詞則是在字首前加上in。

10. highlight 突出、標明

11. photographic memory 過目不忘

12. omit 遺漏、漏寫

13. underscore 下底線
    也寫作understrike、underbar、low line、underdash、underline、low
    dash。

14. approach its conclusion 接近尾聲

💬 練習題

- David has been given the _____ of "playboy" by his friends.
- Please send it to me by using _____.
- Do you know how to _____ in Microsoft Word?
- We lost one million dollars due to his _____.
- The penalty is _____.
- Stop being _____.

- 大衛被他的朋友們貼上花花公子的標籤。
- 請以副本寄給我。
- 你知道怎麼在word檔案裡標明嗎？
- 因為他的不小心，我們損失了一百萬元。
- 這處罰是適當的。
- 別這麼肉麻啦。

💬 解 答

1. label / mark
2. carbon copy
3. highlight
4. inattention
5. appropriate
6. mushy

主題 ⑨ 會議紀錄 Meeting Minutes

職場補給站：拒絕流水帳的會議紀錄

　　許多職場人對於會議紀錄是敬而遠之，能逃就逃，能躲就躲；原因無他，因為會議有時候很冗長，而事後撰寫會議紀錄，也讓人不由想到「回憶錄(memoirs)」。其實這是心理影響生理(The mind-body effect)，因為沒有掌握到撰寫會議紀錄的訣竅，所以產生出的抗拒心理，進而影響撰寫意願與速度。

　　針對如何有效撰寫會議紀錄，以下提供幾項小秘訣與注意事項：

❶ 按照會議大綱(meeting agenda)的順序撰寫。有些公司沒有事前發佈會議大綱的習慣，通常是大家集合、就定位了，由各部門開始報告；但是輪到討論事項時，七嘴八舌，有時候連結論都沒有得出就散會了。這時候會議召集人或單位，最好事前指定負責發佈會議大綱的人，讓參與者知道當天會議流程與討論的事項。會議中也指定會議紀錄人(minutes taker)，在討論事項之後，要提醒會議主持人取得共識或結論，以便載入會議紀錄中。

❷ 在24小時以內撰寫完畢(finish in twenty four hours)。這是一個職場上不成文的規定，會議舉行完畢的24小時之內，必須將會議記錄提供給相關主管、同事等過目；如果對會議記錄有疑問，也應該盡速提出疑問以及正確的資訊，通常也是在24小時以內回覆疑問。

❸ 忌諱流水帳(making a daily journal)的形式。雖然大家都知道這點，但是有些職場新鮮人或者很少撰寫會議紀錄的人，還是會犯這點錯誤，以下有幾點範例可以參考：

- Manager Wang recommends: New product launch should be before the Christmas.　王經理建議：新產品上市應該在聖誕節前。

- Travel destination of staff trip this year is Tokyo. Family allowed joining, and company will pay half.   今年員工旅遊地點是東京。家人可以參加，而且公司會付一半費用。

- After discussion Point 3, members agreed. 討論第三點後，出席者一致同意。

❹ 前一次會議的進度 (progress of previous meeting minutes) 也應該納入。會議中通常會對前次會議尚未完成的進度做報告，所以這部分也應該納入，即使這個議題可能沒有在會議大綱中。

　　總之，每次會議紀錄就是「瞻前顧後」；看看前次的會議紀錄是否有應該跟進的項目，然後將現在或者下個會期之內可能發生的項目，納入討論與結論。

Part
Ten

團購
Group Buying

Unit 01 訂食物飲料 Ordering Food and Drinks

對話 1 Conversation 1

Kirk	Morgan, it's tea time. Would you like some drinks?	摩根，下午茶時間到了。要不要喝點飲料啊？
Morgan	Why not? What do you want to order?	為什麼不呢？你想喝點什麼？
Kirk	I am thinking a cup of Latte.	我在想拿鐵咖啡。
Morgan	Hot or iced? Large or medium? Do you want any sugar?①	熱的還是冰的？大杯還是中杯？甜度呢？
Kirk	Iced and medium, you know I couldn't take any hot drink.	冰的、中杯，我實在受不了熱的飲料。
Morgan	I am the complete opposite.② I want hot bubble tea.	我和你相反。我想要喝熱的珍珠奶茶。
Kirk	Why don't we ask if the other Departments want to join us or not?③ Because the store offers delivery when the order overs three hundred dollars.④	不如問問其他部門要不要一起訂？因為要滿三百元才會外送。
Morgan	Good idea. Ask the Financial Department that has more girls,	好點子。問問女生們比較多的財務部門，應該很快

	should be over three hundred dollars soon. ⑤	就滿三百元了。
Kirk	Would you like some snacks?	要點心嗎？
Morgan	I'll have one chicken-fried steak with spice and sliced. ⑥	那就來分炸雞排，要加辣，還要切。
Kirk	I will have one chicken nugget.	我來份雞塊。
Morgan	OK. I go to ask them.	好啦。我拿去問她們。
Kirk	Thanks a lot.	太感謝你了。
Morgan	Oops, it just occurred to me that this store is closed on each Monday. ⑦	抱歉，我現在才想到，這家每週一公休。
Kirk	What?	什麼？
Morgan	Don't worry about it. We could order from the one at alley.	別擔心啦。巷口那家也可以訂啊。

① no sugar (less sugar) / easy ice (regular ice) / one sugar, one cream

無糖（少糖）╱冰塊少點（正常）╱一包糖、一包奶精

② I don't want to have the same order with you / He always orders something different

我不想和你點的一樣╱他總是和我們點不一樣（一樣）的

③ Do you want to join group buying? / We need five more people to start a group buying

你要加入團購嗎？╱還差五個人就可以團購了

④ The store doesn't delivery today / This order doesn't reach our minimum amount for delivery / Let's order takeout tonight?

今天店家不外送╱這張訂單還不滿外送金額╱今天晚餐叫外賣吧？

⑤ There are more males in Sales Department / There are more males than females in our office

業務部門的男生比較多╱我們公司男多女少

⑥ one house salad with ranch dressing / cream or sugar? / Do you charge for refills?

一份招牌沙拉，淋上田園沾醬╱要奶精還是糖？╱續杯要錢嗎？

⑦ On Wednesday, this store only open for half day / This store only closed during the Chinese New Year

這家店每週三只營業半天╱這家店只有農曆新年休息

對話 2 Conversation 2

Eugene	Hi, Olga. There is a restaurant discount coupon on the group buying website, you want to join us to purchase?	嗨，歐嘉，這個網站正在團購餐廳優惠券，妳要不要加入我們呢？
Olga	What are those special offers? ①	有哪些優惠方案？
Eugene	They offer discount on steak set for four people and hot pot for ten people.	他們提供打折，有牛排套餐四人份還有火鍋十人份。
Olga	Wow, that sounds good. How cheap it is? ②	哇，聽起來不錯喔。有多便宜？
Eugene	Original price is one thousand, now thirty percent off, only three hundred. ③	原價一千元，打三折，現在只要三百元。
Olga	Can I use the coupon anytime?	隨時都可以去消費嗎？
Eugene	No. Only from 11 AM to 6 PM, Monday to Wednesday. ④	沒有喔。只有星期一到三，上午十一點開始到晚上六點前。
Olga	Cannot I go on holidays?	假日不可以去嗎？
Eugene	It says no on coupon terms and conditions. ⑤ You could take a day off or give it to your family.	規定不可以的。妳可以請一天假去，或者讓家人去吃。
Olga	Send it to people as a gift? Like a	當成禮物送給人？像禮券

	gift cereificate?	一樣？
Eugene	Yes. Isn't it a great idea?	對呀。很棒的點子吧？
Olga	Let me think about it. What are the other limitations? ⑥	讓我想想。還有什麼限制？
Eugene	Not really. Or you can join the group buying of this egg roll gift box.	沒有了。或者妳可以團購蛋捲禮盒。
Olga	Well, it sounds more interesting. Does it have fewer limitations?	嗯，好像有趣多了。限制比較少了吧？
Eugene	Yes, they even provide home delivery. ⑦	是的，還可以宅配到家。
Olga	Great, I am in.	太好了，我加入。

實用應答小撇步 2

① While supplies last / 50 percent off during promotional period / but five get one free

這個優惠方案數量有限，售完為止／優惠期間半價優待／買五送一

② Do you offer a discount? / How much discount will I get? / Not cheap enough

有折扣嗎？／我可以獲得多少折扣？／不夠便宜

③ promotion price / twenty percent off offer is valid until seventh, July

優惠價／七月七日前打八折

④ only can come on normal days (weekdays) / only can use it on National Holidays / only can use it during discount period

只有平日可以使用／只有國定假日可以使用／只有在折扣期間可以使用

⑤ Please order after read coupon terms carefully / This coupon against company's sales policies

請詳閱優惠券條款規定後再訂購／這張優惠券違反了公司的銷售規定

⑥ This coupon with no use limitations / This travel tour has many limitations

這張優惠券無使用限制／這個旅遊行程有很多限制

⑦ only can pick up in store / only accept wait in line / only accept pre-order

只能到店取貨／只接受現場排隊／只接受事先預約

單字與句型

1. bubble tea *n.* 珍珠奶茶
   bubble是泡泡的意思，在此是用形容粉圓的外觀像泡泡一樣圓。也可以寫
   成pearl milk tea，pearl就是珍珠的意思，或boba milk tea，波霸奶茶。

2. chicken-fried steak 炸雞排
   也可以寫成deep fried chicken breast。其他中式小吃的英文有：

   stinky tofu 臭豆腐　oyster omelet 蚵仔煎　rice tube pudding 筒仔米糕
   salty rice pudding 碗糕　pigs blood cake 豬血糕　fried white radish
   patty 蘿蔔糕　Taiwanese meatballs 肉圓　tenpura 天婦羅

3. chicken nugget 雞塊
   其他速食點心的英文單字有：

   onion rings 洋蔥圈　milk shake 奶昔　hash browns 薯餅

   snack wrap 捲餅　French fries 薯條

4. group buying 團購
   也可以寫成group purchasing、collective buying。

5. takeout *n.* 外送、外賣
   takeaway則是打包外帶的意思。

6. ranch *n.* 田園醬
   各式沾醬的英文：

   creamy Italian 義大利奶油醬　Thousand Island 千島醬

   tasty sesame vinaigrette 風味芝麻油醋醬

7. restaurant discount coupon 餐廳優惠券
   旅遊優惠券寫作travel discount coupon。

8. terms and conditions 條款與條件
9. gift certificate 禮券

💬 練習題

- Check out our _____ including theatre tickets, attractions, eating out and more.
- Please give me one _____ and _____.
- I got ten _____ from my company.
- Please read _____ carefully before you sign it.

- 點選我們的<u>優惠方案</u>，包含電影票、景點入場券、外出用餐優惠以及更多方案。
- 請給我一份<u>雞塊</u>和<u>珍珠奶茶</u>。
- 公司送給我十張<u>餐廳優惠券</u>。
- 在你簽名之前請小心閱讀<u>條款與條件</u>。

💬 解 答

1. special offers
2. chicken nugget, bubble tea / pearl milk tea / boba milk tea
3. restaurant discount coupons
4. terms and conditions

Unit 02 團購商品 Products

對話 1 Conversation 1

Isabella	Hi, Nigel. What you staring at the screen for?	嗨，奈傑爾。你盯著螢幕看什麼呢？
Nigel	I am thinking of buying this bottle of wine. ①	我在考慮買這瓶葡萄酒。
Isabella	Let me see. Wow, original price is two thousand and promotional price is six hundred! I would love to buy one of them.	讓我也看看。哇，原價兩千元，促銷價六百元！我也想買一瓶呢。
Nigel	Really? Then, let's buy together.	真的嗎？那我們一起團購吧。
Isabella	But there is only two of us, how to do group buy? If we can find more people, maybe we can get more discounts. ②	只有兩個人怎麼團購呢？找更多人優惠更多吧。
Nigel	How about I write to the retailer and ask them how many people for a group buy.	不如我寫信問店家，需要多少人以上才能團購。
Isabella	Sounds good. I will go to ask for more people. I am familiar with	好呀。我來找人。我和資訊部、會計部的人都很

	colleagues in IT and Accounting Departments. ③	熟。
Nigel	It's better that we shop with the whole company! They probably offer large order discounts. ④	最好全公司一起買！他們應該有提供大量訂購的折扣。
Isabella	This will rely on you to talk with the retailer.	這個就要靠你和店家去談了。
Nigel	It will be wonderful if we two could get a complimentary gift. ⑤	最好我們兩個可以獲得免費贈品。
Isabella	How about a bottle of free wine?	不如一瓶免費的葡萄酒怎麼樣？
Nigel	Only one, it's too cheap. You know, we have one thousand and two hundred employees.	才一瓶，太小氣了。我們公司有一千兩百名員工耶。
Isabella	If each person ordered one bottle, then it's one thousand and two hundred bottles. Wow, it is really something.	要是一人訂一瓶，也有一千兩百瓶。哇，的確不得了喔。
Nigel	It is. So I think it's really cheap for one or two bottles of wine.	是呀。所以我想一兩瓶贈品太小氣了。
Isabella	You are right. OK, we'll rely on you for the negotiation. ⑥	那倒是。好吧，靠你去洽談了。

實用應答小撇步 1

① Did you decide to buy it? / He couldn't make up his mind to buy this product / My husband (wife) doesn't allow me to buy

妳決定要買了嗎？／他無法下定決心買這項商品／我先生（太太）不讓我買

② Buy more, save more / Buy more to get more discount

買越多，省越多／買越多，折扣越多

③ I don't know him very well / I have known him for a long time

我和他不是很熟／我認識他已經很久了

④ We don't offer large order discount / There will be bulk order discount if you order over two hundred pieces

我們沒有提供大量訂購的折扣／要訂兩百個以上，才有大量折扣

⑤ It'd better this trip can take place / They'd better provide free trial packs / It'd better have discounts

最好這趟旅行可以成行／最好有提供免費試用包 / 最好有折扣

⑥ We rely on you for this negotiation / The successful bargaining relied on David's hard working / This is the fruits of everybody's hard labor

這次談判就靠你了／這次議價的成功都靠大衛的努力／這是靠大家努力的成果

對話 **2** Conversation **2**

Douglas	Hi, Juliana. How about your proposal writing?	嗨，茱莉安娜。提案寫得怎麼樣？
Juliana	Almost done.	快要完工了。
Douglas	How many times you have rewrite this? Your boss just found fault with everything. ①	妳修改幾次了？妳主管真是愛找碴。
Juliana	He is really changeable. By the way, we are going to join a group buying of heaters, and we are wondering if you would like to join with us?	他是真的很善變。對了，我們要一起團購電暖器，我們想問你是不是有興趣加入我們？
Douglas	The winter is coming, isn't it? Yes, why not?	冬天要到了，不是嗎？好呀，為何不呢？
Juliana	That's great!	太好了！
Douglas	How much for one heater?	一台多少錢？
Juliana	We did the calculation, each person has to buy three heaters and it's six hundred and ninety dollars for each one. ②	我們算過，一個人要買三台，一台是六百九十元。
Douglas	Why I need to buy three of them? I live alone.	為什麼要買三台呢？我一個人住耶。
Juliana	You can send them to your	可以送給親戚、好友，或

	relatives, friends or even parents.③	者你父母。
Douglas	It's a good idea, but...	這主意是很好，但是⋯⋯
Juliana	You see. We only have five people and the minimum order quantity is fifteen, so... ④	是這樣的。我們只有五個人，而最低門檻是要買十五台，所以⋯⋯
Douglas	Then it should be we call our relatives or friends and make them join this group buying.	那麼應該是我們各自去號召親戚、朋友們一起加入這個團購。
Juliana	We tried, but with limited success. ⑤	我們試過了，但是成效有限。
Douglas	Let me try it, just give me few days to decide. ⑥	讓我來試試看吧，給我幾天的時間決定。
Juliana	It is until next Tuesday. ⑦	這個活動只到下週二喔。

實用應答小撇步 2

① His boss is possessive / My boss is a real pain in the ass / Are your boss a nosey one?

他的主管控制慾很強／我的主管很機車／你的主管是一個管很多的人嗎？

② Each customer is limited to four tickets / Each family can join only one time / Employees and their immediate family members are not allowed to participate in the promotion

一人限購四張／一個家庭只能參加一次／公司員工與直屬親屬不得參加本次促銷活動

③ Can send to clients collaboration over one year / Can donate to a Non-Profit Organization / Complimentary- not for sale

可以送給合作一年以上的客戶／可以捐贈給非營利機構／贈品禁止轉售

④ The maximum order amount is one hundred / We need at least one thousand "Like"

最多可以訂一百個／我們需要至少要有一千個人按「讚」

⑤ I have done (tried) my best / Do your best and let God do the rest!

我已經盡力了／盡人事，聽天命！

⑥ I still cannot decide / She is still thinking / He gives up

我還無法決定／她還在考慮／他放棄了

⑦ This campaign is ongoing / This event has ended

這個活動正在進行中／這個活動已經結束了

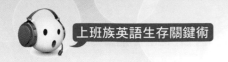
💬 單字與句型

1. promotional price　促銷價
2. retailer *n.*　零售店家
3. large order discounts　大量訂購折扣
   也可以寫作bulk order discount，bulk是批量的意思。
4. complimentary *adj.*　免費的
5. cheap *adj.*　小氣的
   同義詞還有a pinch-penny、stingy、miserly。

   The employer is a pinch-penny.　老闆是個鐵公雞。
6. something *n.*　了不起的事物
   類似用法還有：To go from Nobody to Somebody（從無名小卒到大人物）。
7. trial pack　試用包
   trial還有試驗、考驗的意思。
8. bargaining　討價還價、議價
   bargaining power of buyers / customers，買家／消費者的議價能力。

   名詞為bargain，有議價、合約、買賣、便宜貨的意思。
9. found fault with everything　愛找碴、雞蛋裡挑骨頭、吹毛求疵
10. changeable *adj.*　善變的、變化多端的
    The weather is changeable recently.　最近天氣變化多端。
11. minimum order quantity　最低訂購數量
    又簡稱MOQ。
12. possessive　控制慾的、佔有的
13. pain in the ass　機車、討人厭
    ass（屁股）可以替換成butt（臀部）。本句是形容令人感到十分不舒服、不愉快的人事物；猶如痔瘡，不除不快。引申應用在中文流行語上。

💬 練習題

- David bought the new product to give it a _____.
- To help someone who needs help is _____ to this world.
- My boyfriend is _____.
- It is a good _____.
- You are always trying to _____ with me!
- David is a _____.

- 大衛買了這個新產品試用。
- 幫忙有需要幫助的人對這個世界來說是一件很了不起的事。
- 我的男友很小氣。
- 這是一個很划算的買賣/這是一個便宜貨。
- 你總是想找我碴！
- 大衛真的是很機車。

💬 解　答

1. trial
2. something
3. cheap / a pinch-penny / stingy / miserly
4. bargain
5. find fault
6. pain in the butt / ass

Unit 03 規劃公司旅遊 Corporate Travel Planning

對話 1 Conversation 1

Micky	Do you have a minute, Roger?	羅傑，現在有空嗎？
Roger	Sure, why? You want to discuss the group travel thing now?	有啊，怎麼了？要討論團體旅遊的事情了嗎？
Micky	Yes. I am truly sorry that I leave work early yesterday.[①]	是啊。很抱歉我昨天提早下班。
Roger	It's OK. So, let's go to the meeting room.	沒關係啦。那我們到會議室去吧。
Micky	Sure. I already booked it.[②]	好的。我已經預約使用時間了。
	(At meeting room)	(在會議室裡)
Roger	First, I would like to know the reply from travel agent.	首先，我想先知道一下旅行社的回覆。
Micky	The employees could be divided into four groups. [③] One of the groups has nineteen people.	員工可能會分成四個團。其中一個團人數達十九人。
Roger	Did they explain why they need to do like this?	他們有解釋為什麼要這樣做嗎？

Micky	Because they count in tens, nine people cannot be a group either equally divided. ④	因為旅行社以十人為一單位，九人無法獨立成團也無法均分。
Roger	This is strange. The other three groups only have ten people.	真是太奇怪了。其他三個團只有十個人。
Micky	I know it sounds unreasonable. ⑤ We have to cooperate with the travel agent because time is of the essence.	我知道聽起來很不合理。但是時間緊迫，我們只好配合旅行社。
Roger	All right, then. How about the discount?	好吧。折扣的事情呢？
Micky	Because the departure date is holiday, so they will charge us more. For each person, it is five hundred more. However, we will get five percent off if we pay the deposit within a week. ⑥	因為出團時間剛好是假日，旅行社還會多收團費。一人多五百元。然而，只要在一週內付訂金，可以打九五折。
Roger	I hope that everybody can accept that. How about the payment method?	希望大家可以接受。付款方式呢？
Micky	The travel agent can accept cash or remittance. ⑦	旅行社可以接受現金或匯款。
Roger	OK, then. We will check the progress again with each other tomorrow.	好的，明天我們再彼此確認一下這件事的進度。

實用應答小撇步 1

① He will be away on official business / I will not come to the office this afternoon after meeting clients / Do you take this morning off?

他今天要出公差半天／我下午和客戶會面完就不進公司了／你今天上午都請假嗎？

② Please help to order lunch box for fifty people / Please make a restaurant reservation for the dinner party / Could you help to buy two movie tickets of group buying?

請幫忙訂五十人份的便當／請你預約聚餐的餐廳／可以請你幫我買團購的電影片兩張嗎？

③ Could be divided into five routes / Please break down into six groups / Do we need to divide into that many groups?

可能會分成五條路線／請分成六組／有需要分成那麼多組嗎？

④ Please make a group of nine people / Here can only accommodates up to eight people / Three people sit in a row

請以九人為一組／這裡最多只能容納八個人／一排坐三個人

⑤ You cannot be reasonable with him / This is illogical / It does (doesn't) make sense

你無法和他講道理／這不合邏輯／（不）合情合理

⑥ Must pay the balance payment when the products are ready to delivery / The final two hundred dollars is due upon registration with the balance due 30 days prior to the course commencement

產品運送前，必須繳清尾款／開課前30天要付清剩下的200元

⑦ I don't think you can accept the fact / This is the best of both worlds solution / The client cannot accept the way we handled it at all

我不認為你可以接受這件事實／這是兩全其美的解決方法／客戶十分不能接受我們的處理方式

對話 2 Conversation 2

Stephanie	Cecilia, how are things coming along? ①	西西莉亞，事情進行得怎麼樣？
Cecilia	Hi, Stephanie. Right, about staff travel , the travel agent provided two opinions for us to. ②	嗨，史黛芬妮。是的，關於員工旅遊，旅行社提供了兩套方案給我們選擇。
Stephanie	What's the difference? ③	有什麼不同的地方嗎？
Cecilia	Different attractions, and different dining options.	參觀的景點不同，還有用餐地點也不一樣。
Stephanie	I am all ears.	說來聽聽。
Cecilia	Option A lets us dine in Michelin-starred restaurant once, but arranges only four attractions. ④	A方案提供一次米其林星級的餐廳，參觀的景點只有四處。
Stephanie	And option B?	B方案呢？
Cecilia	All dining at Chinese restaurants. Attractions are more than option A, there are eight of them.	都是吃中國餐館。參觀的景點比較多，有八處。
Stephanie	Well, it's pretty troublesome. Let's put on vote. ⑤	嗯，傷腦筋。不如投票決定吧。
Cecilia	Great idea! I send everybody an E-Mail right now.	好主意。我現在就發 E-Mail給大家。
Stephanie	We are going to departure from the Company, aren't we? ⑥	都是從公司出發沒錯吧？

Cecilia	Yes, we are. The travel agent will drive us to Kaohsiung International Airport. This is the special offer from group buying.	對。旅行社會載我們到小港機場。這是團購的優惠。
Stephanie	Isn't the tip included?	小費是不是不含在費用裡？
Cecilia	No, we need to pay extra for tips to our tour guide and driver every day. [7] It is one thousand a day from each of us.	沒錯，每天的導遊和司機小費都要另外支付。我們每個人一天要付一千元。
Stephanie	It would be better if this is also included in the special offer from group buying.	要是這個也包括在團購優惠裡就好了。

實用應答小撇步 2

① How does it go? / How is it going?

進行得如何？／進行得怎麼樣？

② I made three proposals on marketing meeting / I suggest that each of us comes out one proposal

行銷會議上我提了三個方案／我提議我們每個人想一個方案

③ It makes no difference to me / It seems not so much difference

我看不出來有什麼不同／好像沒有太大的不同

④ C Hotel offers children under the age of 18 can stay for free / Taiwan Railway Administration provides passengers who take kids for a family vacation trip with fifty percentage off on their tickets

C飯店提供18歲以下的孩童免費住宿／台鐵提供參加家庭假期的孩童乘客一律五折票價優惠

⑤ Let's draw lots / Heads or tails?

抽籤決定好了／丟銅板決定吧？

⑥ Please gather in the gallery lobby on the first floor / Where is the gathering place? / We must departure from Taoyuan International Airport

請在一樓的大廳集合／集合地點在哪裡？／我們必須從桃園機場出發

⑦ Tip to restaurant is fifteen percentage of your food and beverage bill / How much should I tip? / It's no need to leave a tip

餐廳的小費是食物與酒水帳單的15%／我該給多少小費？／不需要給小費

單字與句型

1. group travel　團體旅遊
   個人旅遊則是personal travel。

2. travel agent　旅行社

3. count in tens　以十為一個單位

4. equally divided　平均分配、均分
   The money can be divided equally between your children.
   這筆錢可以平均分配給你的孩子們。

5. time is of the essence　時間就是關鍵、時間緊迫
   essence是精華、本質、要素的意思。

6. deposit　訂金、保證金、押金
   也有儲蓄、沉澱物的意思；動詞和名詞同形。動詞則有把⋯存入、寄存、沉澱的意思。

7. payment method　付款方式

8. remittance _n._　匯款

9. be away on official business　因公外出

10. lunch box　便當、午餐盒

11. accommodate _v._　容納
    名詞為accommodation，是宿舍、船位、駐紮的意思。

12. illogical _adj._　不合邏輯
    相反詞則為logical，合邏輯的。

13. balance payment　尾款
    也可以寫作final payment。頭期款則是down payment。

14. best of both worlds　兩全其美的

15. Michelin-starred restaurant(s)　米其林星級餐廳

16. family vacation　家庭假期

練習題

- Some of his arguments are _____ .
- There's a big package of things they have to do and _____ .
- You can _____ your bags at the counter.
- The buyer doesn't satisfied with the _____ which we suggested.
- A prompt _____ would be appreciated

- 他的論點有些並不合邏輯。
- 有一大堆事情要做，而時間就是關鍵（把握時間趕緊做事）。
- 你可以先將行李寄存在櫃台。
- 買方不滿意我們建議的付款方式。
- 請盡速匯款。

解　答

1. illogical
2. time is of the essence
3. deposit
4. payment methods
5. remittance

主題 ⑩ 團購 Group buying

職場補給站：上班族瘋團購

　　一提起團購，許多人會忍不住臉紅心跳、手心冒汗，一副躍躍欲試的模樣。不可諱言，團購確實增添了許多辦公室的樂趣，一大群人分享著美食、旅遊優惠，價格比單買時便宜好多；其實，這不就是彰顯團購原創的精神嗎？

　　根據維基百科(Wikipedia)上對團購的描述，"…offers products and services at significantly reduced prices on the condition that a minimum number of buyers would make the purchase."，顯示團購的幾個要件；第一，可以是買產品或買服務、第二明顯地降價（較低的價格）、第三，要有一定數量的參與者（最低門檻人數）。而台灣針對團購族群所做的統計也指出，近六成上班族是團購的客群，而且集中在已婚人妻女性(married females)。

　　團購商品或服務，例如，美甲服務(nail beauty service)、美髮沙龍服務(hair beauty salon service)，可能存在一些陷阱或注意事項：

❶ 使用期限(expiration)。因為價格比平常便宜許多，商家如何確保利潤呢？答案就在平日促銷這件事上。商家將假日的人潮分散到平日來，滿足可以在平日出來消費的顧客需求，也分散了經營風險（假日如果人擠，會嚇跑不想等待的客人）。要注意的是，消基會曾經秘密訪查過一些商家，發現店家會拒絕購買團購票券的客人進門消費，明明還有空位，卻表明沒有位子；等到使用期限到了，用團購低價買到票券的客人其實沒有機會享受服務。客人反成了冤大頭(suckers)。

❷ 價格灌水(irrigation)。同樣出自消基會的消息，有商家對於放到團購網上

販售的商品，在市場上並無相同的產品以及定價，所以難以判斷其市場價值，變成商家說原價是多少就是多少的羅生門(Rashomon effect)。當然打折下來，消費者買到的「優惠價」是不是真的優惠，也見仁見智。曾經消基會就因為價格灌水事件，開罰過三家知名團購網站。

❸ 團購套餐折扣陷阱(group buying dispute)。有時候低價買到的餐廳美食，份量會縮水一半，旅遊行程則是大多還要自費；最好的自保方式就是貨比三家不吃虧(Shop around before you buy)。

　　其實，團購不只是撿便宜，辦公室有了它，也增進了同事之間情感，甚至是藉機和上司「套近乎、套交情」的一個好藉口。如果你剛好就是團購發起人，有些事項也要留意；首先，確保需要知道這個團購活動的同事、長官們都知道（言下之意，不想讓某些同事或主管知道的話，也要懂得保密）。再者，確保你都清楚了團購的條款與限制(terms and conditions)，以便回答同事們對活動的疑問。如果上述情況都沒有問題了，就可以開心享受團購的樂趣了！

好書報報－生活系列

愛情之酒甜而苦。兩人喝，是甘露；
三人喝，是酸醋；隨便喝，要中毒。

精選出偶像劇必定出現的**8o**個情境，
每個情境－必備單字、劇情會話訓練班、30秒會話教室
讓你跟著偶像劇的腳步學生活英語會話的劇情，
輕鬆自然地學會英語!

作者：伍羚芝
定價：新台幣349元
規格：344頁 / 18K / 雙色印刷

全書中英對照，介紹東西方節慶的典故，
幫助你的英語學習－學得好、學得深入!

用英語來學節慶分為兩大部分－東方節慶&西方節慶

每個節慶共**7**個學習項目：
節慶源由－簡易版、精彩完整版＋實用單字、閱讀測驗、
習俗放大鏡、實用會話、常用單句這麼說、互動單元...

作者：Melanie Venekamp、陳欣慧、倍斯特編輯團隊
定價：新台幣299元
規格：304頁 / 18K / 雙色印刷

用現有的環境與資源，為自己的小寶貝
創造一個雙語學習環境；讓孩子贏在起跑點上!

我家寶貝愛英文，是一本從媽咪懷孕、嬰兒期到幼兒期，
會常用到的單字、對話，必備例句，
並設計單元延伸的互動小遊戲以及童謠，
增進親子關係，也讓家長與孩子一同學習的參考書!

作者：Mark Venekamp & Claire Chang
定價：新台幣329元
規格：296頁 / 18K / 雙色印刷 / MP3

好書報報－職場系列

BEST BOOKS
Best Publishing

結合流行英語，時下必學的行銷手法與
品牌管理概念，讓你完全掌握行銷力！

全書分為**6**大章，共**46**組情境
★ 背景介紹＋實用對話
★ 練習題：中英對照，學習事半功倍
★ 相關詞彙：必備常用單字及片語＋文法加油站
★ 知識補給站：分析行銷策略＋重點訊息彙整
★ 10篇會議要點：對話急救包＋要點提示

題材充實新穎，增加語言學習和專業知識的深度！
行銷人要看，商管學院師生更不可錯過！

作者：胥淑嵐
定價：新台幣349元
規格：352頁／18K／雙色印刷

旅館的客戶為數不少來自不同國家，
因而說出流利的旅館英語，是旅館人員
不可或缺的利器，更是必備的工具!

特別規劃**6**大主題 **30**個情境 **120**組超實用會話
中英左右對照呈現對話內容，閱讀更舒適！
精選好學易懂的key word＋音標＋詞性，學習效率加倍！
隨書附有光碟小幫手，幫助你熟悉口語、訓練聽力！

從預約訂房、入住，到辦理退房，
設計各種工作時會面臨到的場景，
提供各種專業會話訓練，英語溝通零距離!

作者：Mark Venekamp & Claire Chang
定價：新台幣469元
規格：504頁／18K／雙色印刷／MP3

上班族英語生存關鍵術

作　　　者／胥淑嵐

封 面 設 計／King Chen

內 頁 構 成／菩薩蠻有限公司

發 行 人／周瑞德

企 劃 編 輯／丁筠馨

校　　　對／丁筠馨・劉俞青・徐瑞璞

印　　　製／世和印製企業有限公司

初　　　版／2014 年 2 月

定　　　價／新台幣 329 元

出　　　版／倍斯特出版事業有限公司

電　　　話／（02）2351-2007

傳　　　真／（02）2351-0887

地　　　址／100 台北市中正區福州街 1 號 10 樓之 2

E　m　a　i　l／best.books.service@gmail.com

總 經 銷／商流文化事業有限公司

地　　　址／新北市中和區中正路 752 號 7 樓

電　　　話／（02）2228-8841

傳　　　真／（02）2228-6939

國家圖書館出版品預行編目(CIP)資料

上班族英語生存關鍵術 / 胥淑嵐著. ── 初版. ──
臺北市 ： 倍斯特, 2014.02
面 ； 公分
ISBN 978-986-90331-0-7(平裝)

1.英語 2.職場 3.會話

805.188　　　　　　　　　　　　103000347